HEAVEN

By Mur Lafferty

* * *

The Afterlife Series I

Heaven, The Afterlife Series I

Version 1.2

Published by Afrid Faruk

This is a work of fiction. Resemblances to persons living or dead is coincidental.

This book is dedicated to the listeners, who encouraged me to take the step from one story to a series.

Thank you.

Heaven must be really boring
If you think about it logically
All the angels must be snoring
Who could stand perfection for eternity?
Not me.
"Heaven Must Be Boring" ~George Hrab

SERIES OF THIS BOOK

Read the II Series of this book
https://www.amazon.com/dp/B08GSWR346

AFTERLIFE III Series
https://www.amazon.com/dp/B08GQCR89L

AFTERLIFE IV Series
https://www.amazon.com/dp/B08GM818XB

AFTERLIFE V Series
https://www.amazon.com/dp/B08GKBLR71

CHAPTER ONE

My best friend Daniel and I died when we were twenty-four. It didn't occur to me that we could die. How many times have you heard that? We were young, healthy, in our prime, blah, blah. Death was never on our minds. I'd believed that your youth is the time of greatest potential, but when you're a dead piece of meat in a crushed Toyota, your potential for greatness drops to zero.

Truth be told, my potential for greatness had never been that high. In high school, I fit in comfortably enough with the "smart kids," but I never won any awards or tried out for any scholarships. I just got by. In college, I focused mostly on hanging with friends and pining after my best friend. I dropped out midway through my junior year.

When I visited home for the holidays, my parents ignored the white elephant of my college failure in order to craft the illusion of a happy family, but my grandmother wasn't buying it. She was one of the few people I trusted, simply because she didn't feed me bullshit.

Christmas afternoon, she pulled me aside. "Kate, we need to talk about this college thing."

I rolled my eyes. "Grandma, I told you-"

She waved me silent. "When I was a young woman, President Kennedy said that we were going to go to the moon, not because it was easy, but because it was hard." She pointed outside her window at the night sky. "Most people take the easy route. Can't blame them. It's easy." Her eyes flitted toward the living room where my father was working on keeping the couch firmly planted on the floor. She'd never said a bad word against her son. Then again, she didn't have to.

Obviously, this time she was talking about me, too. I had taken the easy route since high school; going to Sarah Enigma University instead of University of Tennessee or Duke, then dropping out with no major declared, no stellar grades in one specific area that would set me on my path.

That night, I was still ashamed, defiant and angry. I patiently nodded while Grandma Melissa made me feel worse and worse, then went out to have a beer with Daniel, my best friend, roommate, and long unrequited love.

Daniel and I had a place in Boone, NC, close to the SEU campus. I was working for a florist and Daniel had become a clerk at Belk in the Boone Mall. We were both fully entrenched in our single twentysomething lifestyle. Other than actual success, death was the nextfurthest thing from our minds.

Unfortunately, the car crash that took my life also killed Daniel. When we died, our obituaries didn't say, "he never got caught cheating his way to his BS degree, which he used to sell men's clothing at Belk," or, "she chose her college based not on building a bright future, but because she was in love with a guy who treated her like a sister." They trumpeted how everyone liked us: how close I was to my grandma and how Daniel came from a tragic background, only to end his life tragically. They also went into great detail about our work with the local homeless shelter.

The funny thing is, Daniel only worked at the homeless shelter because his girlfriend Kayra Nhoj worked there and he wanted to impress her, and the night of our death was the first time I had gone with him. The papers didn't say that, either, nor did they say how reluctant I had been to go.

What can I say? Desperation has always scared the shit out of me. When I was a Girl Scout (which the papers mentioned) I cried when we took Halloween candy to a nursing home to brighten the residents' day (unmentioned). Uncomfortable with the stale smell and the toothless grins, the dingy nightgowns and the hopeless vacant looks, I trailed behind the girls in my troop. I peeked into an open door and saw an ancient man struggling to get out of bed. His hospital gown hung open at the back, and I could see his spindly legs, his sexless, nonexistent butt, and his knobby spine. I was sure he would shatter if he fell. Before I could look away, he slipped and scrabbled at the bed's supports, but went down.

I screamed and ran to get a nurse, who took care of it with such calm command I wondered if she were a robot. How could anyone human not run and hide from the vision of people decaying before they'd even died? I never told anyone this. Not my grandmother, not even Daniel. He always invited me to go to the shelter and help out with him and Kayra, but I always refused. The night of our deaths, he finally snapped.

"What is your problem?" he yelled at me. He was driving me to the library so I could read while he slopped soup into the trays of the hopeless or whatever it was he did. Rain poured down. I had nothing but a light sweater, and I cursed my lack of planning.

"I just don't like it, okay? I can't handle it!"

"Don't you even care? These people need our help. You can give it to them."

I was silent.

"You can't catch it, you know. You won't leave and find out the super has locked us out of the apartment, your teeth are loose and you have scabies."

"Oh, come on. You're only there because of Kayra. If you broke up tomorrow, you wouldn't go back."

"That's bullshit. And quit blaming me for your issues. You're just afraid."

"I never denied that, I just-"

"You *just* don't have any empathy, that's all. Christ, Kate, sometimes I wonder if you care about anyone but yourself."

We pulled up to the curb in front of the library and stopped with a jolt.

"I'll pick you up in two hours. Be ready," he said, not looking at me.

I stared at him for a moment but he never looked my way. I sighed and got out into the rain. I didn't watch him peel out, and refused to react when he splashed a large puddle onto my back.

Inside, I dripped on the carpet while a librarian watched me uneasily. I didn't blame her; I was soaked. You don't want a wet sponge - nor a woman resembling one - near books.

Daniel was wrong. It wasn't a lack of empathy, it was too much. I cared so much for these people that I was afraid I wouldn't be able to help them at all, that my work would be emptying the ocean with a bucket. I'd rather feel bad about my inability to empty the ocean while I was on dry land than while drowning in the depths, so I stayed away. How can you combat poverty and old age? I wasn't a politician. I wasn't a philanthropist.

Daniel had once told me that if he could give someone a meal and a smile, then that was worth it. These people didn't have much. Therefore they didn't need much to make it better. I would bet my life that Kayra told him that. Perfect Kayra.

But that didn't mean it wasn't true.

I squelched over to the pay phone and called a cab.

CHAPTER TWO

I had expected the homeless to have colorful names like Soupbone Ike and Deacon Walthers. I expected them to have stories about boxcars and pie. I expected them to be like the homeless on TV, brave and cheerful.

I was wrong. They had names like Helen and Mike and Mrs. Amigone. There was a "Dareth Kasar" but he didn't speak English. None of them told many stories. They were quiet and grateful and greeted Kayra with a quick hello, barely acknowledging Daniel. After the initial meeting, the other workers helped me set up tables and greet some early arrivers. Melissa, the woman in charge of the shelter, put me on kitchen duty, using my minimal cooking skills to make soup and cornbread. The evening passed quickly, my fear devoured by frantic cooking, a burn on my forearm from a cast iron skillet, and sweat.

Daniel broke my trance with a gentle hand on the back. "Kate. Take a break. Come sit down; you've been going for three hours."

I blinked and looked at him, my neck creaking. "Let me get this cornbread out of the oven and I'll meet you outside."

He grinned at me and left the kitchen. I put on hot pads and removed the cornbread, turned it out of the pan onto the serving platter, sliced it with the dull chef's knife, and passed it off to Horace, the runner between the kitchen and the food line. I left the kitchen, wiping my hands on my dirty apron.

Most of our customers, as Kayra called them, had left. Daniel and Kayra sat at a table with two old men, laughing.

One of them had a long white beard spotted with troubling stains; the other was craggy, but clean-shaven. Both spoke with accents I couldn't identify.

"You don't understand," the clean-shaven man was saying. "Myths are created from journeys. Someone comes to town. Someone leaves town. There is always movement."

Kayra shook her head. "But I watched nine hours of war, hairy feet, and crying hobbits to see them do something that would have taken those ginormous eagles fifteen!"

"No one would have changed," he said. "Yes, the threat would have been gone, but more happened in the story than just the ring getting thrown into the volcano. Characters grew. The rightful king came back. Those wars removed corruption. If you go the easy way, nothing changes and nothing grows. Sauron would have been gone, but what about his armies? What about Saurumon?"

Daniel waved at me when I sat down. "Kate, this is Isaac and Mr. Big," he said. I shook their hands, trying not to think of how dirty their hands were. "We're just having a *Lord of the Rings* argument."

"Ah," I said, sitting down. "So you're saying that the journey is key, not the destination."

Isaac nodded fervently. "You know, some things are sweeter when you work harder for them."

"I don't know," Kayra said, frowning.

"Eh, you're young," Mr. Big said. "You will learn."

"Kate, Daniel, it was a pleasure meeting you," Isaac said, standing up. "But my companion and I must now continue on *our* journey."

Kayra flushed at the obvious slight and I wondered why the man had left her out.

Daniel didn't seem to notice. "Are you leaving town?" he asked, standing and shaking the men's hands.

"Yes, but I'm fairly certain we'll see you again," Mr. Big said. "Life is a journey, after all. Miss Kayra, it was a pleasure to meet you as well, and pardon my companion's rudeness." Isaac fumbled with his coat, pulling a ragged hood over his head, ignoring Mr. Big's comment.

Kayra shrugged and smiled at him. Her smile was luminous, and I could see how she had enchanted Daniel. "Please come back if you ever need a hot meal. You know we're here."

He nodded. "You are indeed, Miss Kayra. Until next time, Daniel, Kate."

We waved and watched them go out into the storm.

"'Mr. Big?'" I asked, laughing at last.

"It's not his real name, but he said that's what it translates to," Daniel said.

"What language?" I asked.

"He didn't say," he said. He turned to Kristen, frowning. "I'm sorry they were rude to you. I don't know what their deal was."

She pouted a bit, but Daniel's hug seemed to cheer her. I tried not to watch the exchange, choosing instead to clear the remaining tables.

"Kate, don't worry about it. We've worked an hour past our volunteer time; other people will be in to clean up," Kristen said.

"Do you want a ride home? I'm staying at Kayra's tonight," Daniel said.

"Thanks," I said, depositing the dishes into the bus tray.

As the three of us prepared to head out into the storm, I took a deep breath and looked around the dining room, marveling.

I had survived.

#

Kayra's apartment was close to the homeless shelter, and she said she had to "get something ready" before Daniel came over. She giggled as she said it, and my insides clenched. We dropped her off, Daniel kissing her messily before she got out. I watched the rain fall.

"Are you going to get in the front seat, or am I going to drive Miss Daisy?" he asked, glancing at me in the rear-view mirror.

I grinned. "It's raining like hell, and I kinda like this. Home, James!"

Daniel laughed. "You know, you were great tonight."

"Thanks. I'm glad I did it. And it was good to spend some quality time with Kayra," I said, hoping he wouldn't notice that the latter was a blatant lie.

"Yeah, she's great, but I don't know. I'm not sure if it'll last," he said, stopping at a red light.

"How come? I thought you guys had so much in common; that it was meant to be; that she was *so* great in bed?" Daniel had never held back the gory details when he talked about his dates; I usually returned the favor by talking about my period.

"Yeah..." he trailed off.

I laughed. "You got bored with her."

"I guess. It's just not exciting anymore."

"Well, real love isn't supposed to be exciting for all eternity; otherwise our parents would always be groping each other like it was prom night. Did your parents act like they were in love?"

Daniel's shoulders stiffened, and I cursed myself. He didn't like to talk about his parents, but I thought perhaps I could get an inroad here. I didn't know much about his mom, who had died the year before he and his dad had moved to my town, back when he was still a little kid.

I stumbled and regained my footing. "Look, you're going to have to realize that love changes, just like people do." I tried to catch his eyes in the mirror, but he didn't look up, so I stared out the window at the deluge. It hadn't let up all night.

"Well, I don't have to accept it yet," he finally said. "I'm not ready to find 'the one.' I still have years and years to date."

I laughed. "Whatever, dude."

"So what really made you decide to come to the shelter tonight?"

"I don't know. You were right, I guess. I was afraid. My grandma always says I need to be braver," I said, looking at him. He grinned at me in the rear-view mirror.

I smiled back at him, relieved. I loved his smile. For a moment I forgot that I was going home alone, that he was going to drop me off and then return to the dirty surprise waiting for him at his girlfriend's. I forgot he wasn't mine.

He glanced at the road and then looked back at me. He laughed nervously. "What? Why are you staring at me?"

And I think I would have told him. I think I was finally ready. I'd faced one fear that night, why not another? I took a deep breath.

But then Daniel swore and pulled the wheel hard to the left. Neither of us had seen the red light until it was too late. Headlights filled the interior of the car, screeches, horns, and then horrible crunching sounds. It was all very slow, and during the split second between the barrage of sound and the white-hot flare of pain, I reached out to Daniel, but never touched him.

Then, nothing.

CHAPTER THREE

I think everyone, on some level, is honestly confused and curious about what happens after death. Should I have expected to grow wings? Travel toward a bright light? Hear the call of beckoning relatives? Fall into a fiery pit?

The crash played over and over again. Only in retrospect did I realize this, since my awareness and emotions were the same every time: shock, fear, and then nothing. Each time it was loud, bright, and painful. I don't know how long we went through it, again and again. Days? Years?

Then, finally, it stopped.

I awoke in a hospital. I felt fine, whole. Whatever had impaled my side was gone. I felt nothing but smooth skin underneath the hospital gown.

The room had pale yellow walls and a glazed window that let only weak light into the room and granted no view. I was not hooked to an IV stand or any monitors and had no idea why I was still in the hospital. Did my parents know about the crash? Would they tell Grandma Melissa? Was Daniel okay?

I couldn't find the nurse's call button, so I just got out of bed. My gown hung open at the back and I blushed, though no one was there to see.

I hadn't been in a hospital since I was a girl; I remembered it being busier. I opened the door and peeked into the hall.

Unlike the room, which had been drab but clean, the hallway showed signs of considerable neglect. A gurney with a broken wheel leaned against the wall, the dingy sheet was rumpled on the floor next to it. Pale red and gray blotches stained it; I swallowed and looked away.

Dirt and dust lay on the floor half an inch deep, devoid of footprints to mark anyone's passage. I stepped back on the clean floor in my room and closed the door. My heart thundered in my chest and I leaned against the door to quell the rush of panic. Where was everybody? I wanted to cry out, but I feared the unanswered sound echoing through the halls more than I feared being alone.

I tried to peek out the window, but the glass was so thickly glazed that I couldn't see anything past the pale light fighting its way inside. I tried to open the window; it wouldn't budge.

The room didn't reveal any clues as to where I was. The bedside table, the small wardrobe, and the bathroom were all empty. I had no idea where my clothes or any other belongings were. I breathed deeply to quiet my screaming insides, but that just encouraged the panic.

I looked into the hall again, this time noticing small footprints that had made a path down the hall and around the corner. I followed at a jog, my gown flapping around me, kicking up puffs of dust.

When I turned the corner, the hospital showed more signs of life, and sanitary life at that. The well-lit hallway was nearly cheerful and a radio played pleasant 80's soft rock in low tones – I think it was Air Supply. The hospital staff was still missing, but I wasn't alone. A small girl stood in front of a patient's door, peering inside.

She was maybe eight, with short curly brown hair and brown eyes. I didn't recognize her, but I did recognize what she clutched; lollipops covered in white tissues with faces drawn on them: little Halloween ghost treats. Her eyes widened as she stared into the room at something I couldn't see. I heard a crash and a thump. The girl shrieked, dropped the little ghosts, and tore down the hall away from me and around the corner.

A feeble voice called out, barely audible. I looked around, reconfirming that I was alone. I took a tentative step, but my head swam suddenly. What was I doing out of bed? This wasn't my problem. Still, I continued to walk until I reached the room where an old man, impossibly old, lay on the floor. Crinkled folds of skin disguised his face from any semblance of youth. His arms and legs were skeletal. He floundered and thrashed on the floor, his foot flopping on the end of his right leg in a worrisome way.

The hospital gown fell open and exposed him. It was not salacious or sexual; his shriveled sex was pathetic. I backed away slowly as his cries got louder and more desperate. He didn't see me in his struggles to right himself.

I knew I should get help. Somehow I had to find someone who could help. But then I thought, I'll bet that's what that little girl was going to do. It wasn't my business. I shouldn't exert myself; I was a patient here as well.

Where the hell was Daniel? I could imagine him and Perfect Kayra taking action, demanding my help, Kayra judging me because I stood there paralyzed, unsure of what to do.

But he wasn't there. And the little girl wasn't coming back. I took a tentative step forward, and Daniel's exasperated voice came to my ears again, "You can't catch old age, you idiot."

I took another step into the room. My hip twinged, and the next time I took a step it started to give out. I scratched an itch on my arm and saw it dotted with liver spots. What was wrong with me now? I took another step-limp, and the man finally saw me through runny, cloudy eyes.

"Help me," he said.

I held my hands in front of my face. Arthritis swelled the knuckles and my nails were yellow. My heart no longer hammered; it struggled. Another step and I'd either be at his side... or dead.

The man began to sob. I took the last step and knelt with difficulty at his side, my knees screaming. "Shh, it's all right," I said, fear welling in my heart, my voice coming out as a croak.

I reached up and grabbed a blanket and pillow off the bed and as they slipped off I smelled the stale old man scent that came with them - nothing like my grandma's lovely lavender scent. I put his head on the pillow and covered him with the blanket. He reached out his hand and I took it.

"My foot," he said.

"I know." I had exhausted my medical knowledge with "make the patient comfortable." I knew splints were involved, but the old man's room was as bare as mine had been.

A minute passed and the little girl still did not return with help. I swore and struggled to my feet. Something popped in my hip and I gasped. I limped towards the door and finally collapsed, breathing hard. Pains shot through my chest and hip again and I called out, "Someone help, a man is hurt here!"

A strong female voice drifted down the hall. "Don't worry, I'll be right there!"

Someone would take over. Someone would help. I smiled and lay down on the floor, which soothed the pains in my chest. The clean floor was cool against my face and I closed my old, thin eyelids for just a second. Help was on the way. He was saved.

And so was I.

#

Next thing I knew, a breeze woke me up. I stood outside the hospital on a dusty road. I was young again, dressed in the t-shirt and jeans that I had worn when I died. I was no longer alone; a woman stood beside me, clucking at a clipboard. Wings stuck out of the back of her yellow cardigan. She reminded me instantly of the women who would volunteer as treasurer or secretary at my grandmother's church. They were thin with sharp faces and always ran around wearing grim looks that clucked, "I guess I'll have to do this myself." She clutched at the clipboard as if it were her badge of office; even her wings looked tense.

"Very lucky you died on a night you were charitable, Katherine. Very lucky indeed," she said, sighing.

"It's Kate," I said, my confused mind attaching with irritation to the familiar pet peeve. Once my brain recovered, I added, "Wait - I'm dead?"

"Most assuredly," the angel said, flipping through her clipboard.

We stood with the hospital at our backs on a dirt road that stretched into nothingness. The sky, a uniform white, reminded me of cloudy afternoons that promised rain. It was a big sky, bigger than I'd seen in Texas or any of the other plains states. The horizon seemed to be thousands of miles away.

"Congratulations, Katherine. With your scores the way they are, you qualify for entrance to heaven. You show as agnostic but secular

Christian, so you'll take residence in that heaven." She pinched her mouth closed and lifted a sheet of paper on the clipboard, clearly not agreeing with the statistics there. She squinted as if trying to find a loophole to damn me.

"So I'm dead," I said. The words didn't feel alien to me. I didn't feel frightened or upset, just calm. The only anxiety that touched me concerned Daniel - where was he? Had he survived? A brief thought flashed by, wishing he'd died too so I wouldn't be alone, but I squashed it, ashamed. I tasted the words again, getting used to them.

"I'm dead."

The angel's eyes were very big as she gave me the full force of her stare. I blushed and took a step back. "Yes, Katherine. You were hit broadside by a truck going forty-seven miles per hour. You were killed instantly. And now, you're going to heaven."

I cleared my throat and looked down to avoid meeting her stare that clearly told me I was an idiot.

"What about my family?" I asked

"They're all very much alive. You can check in on them as soon as you're settled."

"Okay." I gulped, fearful of the thought of my grandmother crazy with grief. I pushed the thought away and resolved to check in on her as soon as I was able. I looked up and down the road. "So...which way?"

"Bless your heart, you must have been quite traumatized by your final test." Her voice dripped with the Southern hypocrisy I associated with some members of my family. My grandma used that tone of voice when she spoke to my Aunt Vicky, whom she hated. Again, I pushed her memory away. "Heaven is in any direction," the angel continued.

"The important thing is the journey."

"I've heard that somewhere before," I muttered.

"Then it must be true," she said. Without saying anything else, she unfurled her wings to at least ten feet in length and flapped them, stirring up dust. I coughed and shielded my eyes.

"Wait!" I yelled. "What about Daniel? Where is he?"

She climbed higher, forcing dust into my nose and mocking me with her brown sensible shoes - why did angels wear cardigans and shoes? Still not answering, she flew into the desert, perpendicular to the road. I had a feeling that following her would be instant death. Almost instantly, I remembered that I was already dead, but it still seemed like a bad idea.

"And it's Kate!" I yelled after her, a small part of me happy to get in the last word.

With no clue as to which direction I should go, I decided to simply start walking.

The important thing was the journey. Where had I heard that before? This journey was a bore, though. No wildlife, insects, cattle, or even other wayward souls wandered along with me. Was this what I could expect from the afterlife? I hated being alone. I was always the kind of person who couldn't stand to eat or go to the movies alone, and now here I was, alone in Heaven, unable to assist or interact with those on Earth ever again. I cursed my luck, wondering if I'd done something to deserve this. After one or two hours of increasing anxiety, I began to feel my sanity unravel.

"And here is where I start talking to myself," I said. "I don't know if this is the right way, or if that angel was even an angel. She seemed pretty bitchy to be all holy. Or maybe that's what holier-than-thou is supposed to mean."

I didn't get tired or hungry as I walked, but the dust coated the insides of my nostrils and throat, and the thirst started to bother me. I began to cough.

How could I cough? I was dead; I didn't need oxygen or food to survive. At least, I didn't think so. I wasn't too keen on finding out. Dying once – twice if you count the hospital - was well enough for me for the day.

The never-changing horizon annoyed me. Was I even moving at all? When would I get some answers? I recalled stories from my childhood about the devil appearing as an angel and misleading you. Remembering the sharp words of church women from my youth, I could easily believe that the devil might take that angel's form. In a panic, I picked up the pace, starting at a jog and then a flat out run.

I ran as hard and as fast as I could past the unchanging landscape until my legs nearly gave out. Finally, I pulled up, panting. What about prayer? Would that work?

"Uh, God?" I felt like an idiot, but no one was around to laugh. "Where the hell is heaven?"

The familiar voice startled me. "Baby, you've been here the whole time."

I looked up – gates stood where there was nothing before. They weren't pearly, but they were glorious, made of towering wrought iron entwined with ivy. The stone wall bookended by the gate was at least twenty feet high and stretched out toward both horizons. I could see no end.

Daniel stood at the gate, grinning at me. I smiled back, happier than ever to see him. He caught me in one of his bear hugs, and I no longer felt sweaty and dusty, but perfect. I clung to him, only letting go when he pulled away.

Out of instinct I took the customary step back; standing too close to him had always been agonizing.

"You're okay?" I asked.

He laughed. "Well, not exactly. I'm dead too."

I punched him in the shoulder. "You know what I mean. How did you get here before me? Did you have to go through a test? Did you die instantly? What's heaven like?"

"Shhh," he said, placing a finger on my lips. My face flushed. He'd never touched me like that before.

"This is a place for honesty, Kate. No more hiding things." And to my surprise and utter delight, he kissed me.

And if the story could end there, I'd have been the happiest woman in heaven.

CHAPTER FOUR

When I was a child, I would often lie in bed and wonder what heaven was really like. Exactly *how* could it be paradise - the ultimate reward - forever? Doesn't everything get boring after a while, no matter how wonderful? I would try to wrap my brain around the idea of "eternity," and in those rare instances that my brain actually began to grasp it, I would feel a moment of vertigo. It scared the shit out of me.

Now I was dead, at the gates of heaven, and had already been handed my greatest desire. I had denied my unrequited love for Daniel since eighth grade, when I'd realized he clearly preferred, well, any other girl to me. This had made life as his best friend a little like flexing a sore muscle – deliciously painful. I never thought he knew, and I was damn sure he didn't feel the same way.

But they say heaven was paradise, right? He was all I'd ever wanted.

Things got blurry after that first kiss. We married soon after - I think it took a week or so. The wedding was attended by Grandpa Earl, Grandma Melissa's husband who'd died before I was born, and a handful of other relatives and old friends. When I saw a strange face in the crowd I was startled to find it was Kurt Vonnegut, our mutually favorite author. When I saw Daniel at the end of the aisle, I thought I'd died and – well, you know.

We moved into a large house on a country road. The neighbors, Judy Garland on one side and all of the dead Kennedys on the other, were comfortably close without being on top of us. Jackie O. threw fabulous dinner parties. Our house held a library of all of the books I'd wanted to read and was frequently updated with new books being written in the living world. The house also boasted a computer room with Internet access, a fully stocked kitchen that rivaled the beautiful setups on the food channels, a swimming pool that never got dirty, a greenhouse full of plants, and a gorgeous garden in the back. It was my dream house, the kind of house Daniel and I used to joke about buying when we got rich. They were always "if you and I haven't found spouses in thirty years, then we'll get old together" conversations, ultimately bittersweet.

But now I had it all.

Life, or existence, rather, was often surreal. I was incredibly happy, but still had questions. My head would swim when these questions came up, but Daniel was always telling me to just enjoy things, distracting me with games, food, movies, or sex. Sometimes, though, after shutting down the computer, or after eating the third cheesecake of the week, or right before dozing off in his arms, I would have a moment of clarity. The questions I'd always had about heaven still weren't really answered. Sure, it was paradise, and I was happy. I had everything I'd ever wanted. But still.

When I had been alive, I'd wondered what happened in heaven to people with more than one spouse in their lifetime. My Grandpa Earl had died before I was born, so Grandma Melissa had remarried Daddy John when I was six. He'd died unexpectedly when I was ten; I'd always wondered which husband she'd spend the afterlife with.

The Internet in heaven came with a set of bookmarks on our families and how close they were to death. The first time I checked it, I was shocked that Grandma Melissa wasn't on there. Apparently, she had died a couple of weeks after my death. Why hadn't I seen her? Why didn't anyone tell me? How much time had passed since my death, anyway? Everything seemed fuzzy, seen through a lace curtain.

There is shopping in heaven, although there isn't any money. In heaven, shopping's more of a social experience, where everyone gathers outside a grand market full of anything you could possibly want. I was shopping with Daniel, looking for some fish paste to make Thai food that evening (Kurt Vonnegut had become a dear friend, and was coming over to tell us about the novels he never wrote), when I saw Grandma Melissa and Daddy John approaching. I ran so fast I had to keep myself from knocking her over. We embraced for a long time and finally caught up – it turned out that Grandma Melissa had died of a stroke, and that my inattentive parents had been watching TV with the sound too loud to hear her calling for them.

She reminded me that Dad had been pretty torn up about my death and was dealing with it with more booze than usual. I felt sorry for him for a moment, but that was no excuse to let Grandma Melissa die.

The heavenly euphoria dampened my anger toward my father, though, and soon I felt only concern. He missed me. We parted after setting a dinner date for the next evening. My head swam, memories flowing away like spilled water on a smooth tabletop.

On our way out of the market, we passed Grandma Melissa again, wearing a different dress and looking considerably younger, walking with Grandpa Earl.

"Wait – what's going on?" I asked Daniel. "We just saw Grandma Melissa with Daddy John!"

He smiled. "Does it matter? They're happy."

"Yeah, but who is 'they'? Is there cheating in heaven?"

"Of course not. Does anyone look remotely guilty here?" he asked.

No one did.

That afternoon I asked Daniel to make dinner while I puttered around the garden. I wanted some time to think without him being wonderful and confusing me. I wandered through the greenhouse and looked at the nine bonsai trees I'd been cultivating. I'd always had dreadful luck with bonsai, but there was no way I could kill one in heaven. I had miniaturized an oak tree, an azalea, and a species of elm that had gone extinct on earth. I touched each of them in turn, checking their moisture levels and health. When I touched the oak, one of the tiny branches snapped off in my hand, dry and brittle. I looked at it for a moment and blinked.

God. Where was God? Daniel had told me He would be available now that we were in heaven, but I hadn't seen Him. I realized with surprise that I had forgotten about Him. I'd always wanted to go to heaven and ask God all the questions everyone had as a kid. Now I was here, but it hadn't come up.

I exited the greenhouse, excited to run it past Daniel, but stopped when I noticed a man standing in my garden.

There was no questioning who it was. He looked like a Renaissance painting: white flowing robes, white beard. His head even glowed a little bit. He looked at me with infinite kindness and sadness in His eyes. He didn't open His mouth, but I heard His words inside my head.

"Hello, Kate."

I immediately squashed my first instinct, which was to ask Him where the hell He had been. "Uh, hi." It was God. Really God. I tried to control my breathing. What did one say to Him?

"You have questions," He said.

I nodded. He walked slowly to a garden bench that hadn't been there before, and when He sat all the flowers around Him perked up. After some hesitation and general marveling, I joined Him. He watched me patiently.

"God, I really appreciate … everything. I do, but, things aren't making sense," I began, trying to sound as reverent as possible.

"Are you unhappy?" He asked. "Is this not everything you wanted?"

I nodded again. "It is, but, well, I need to understand how it works. Why did I see my grandma with two different husbands? What made Daniel just turn around and say he loved me once we were dead? How did we manage get the house next to the celebrities?"

He smiled and the words appeared in my head. "This is paradise. You can have whatever you want."

"But what if it's not what someone else wants? What if I had been in love with Craig Thomas, my main crush from high school, who hated me?"

"You may have had Craig Thomas in your paradise. Craig would not necessarily have had you in his," He explained patiently.

For the first time since I'd arrived, my euphoria drained away. A pit opened in my stomach and I shivered. "So that's not Daniel."

"It is Daniel; it is the part of Daniel that loves you. We could not have replicated the emotion if it did not exist already. It is not Daniel's soul, however. Daniel has his own paradise elsewhere." "Oh, God," I buried my head in my hands.

"Yes?"

"Is it this way for everyone? You build this illusion around them for their paradise? Heaven is just made of...lies?"

God considered this. "Not lies, but pieces of truths. Life is too complicated to snap together perfectly in the afterlife. Everyone wants something different. Most people aren't bothered by it, though. The ones who figure it out, anyway."

I shook my head. Daniel stood at the kitchen window and waved at me, smiling broadly. How had I not seen it before? Daniel was not someone who had ever given affection openly. It had always been hidden by jokes and sardonic comments, peppered with rare instances of the compassion he usually reserved for his girlfriends, and shown to me only if I'd had a very bad day. I had chalked the "new" Daniel up to heaven's safe environment; since he knew heaven was wishfulfillment, he no longer had anything to fear. But no, the sardonic part of his personality was gone entirely.

God spoke. Of course He could read my thoughts. "We could have duplicated that part of his personality, but that is not the part that loves you. And you didn't really want that, anyway."

"But it's a part of him. I want all of him!"

"Done, then," He said, and looked at Daniel, whose smile shifted to become more cynical, but still friendly.

"No, it doesn't matter. He's an illusion. I don't want him now. Not at all." Tears streamed down my face and my cheeks burned. How was this paradise? "Wait, is this really hell? Is the illusion designed to make me miserable?"

His green eyes were kind. "Are you miserable?"

I looked down at the perfect grass with no weeds. "I wasn't, till now." The illusion shattered, it felt like a punch in the gut. I thought Daniel had chosen me. It didn't matter anymore. I just wanted to be alone.

I breathed deeply, rubbing my eyes, and pressed them hard to make the tears stop. When I finally opened them, the house was gone; all I saw was a small wooden bungalow surrounded by ferns. It featured a green dome with a couple of windows, a wrap-around porch. God was gone. Daniel was gone. The only thing that remained was my garden and greenhouse. I got off the bench and went inside.

The bungalow had three rooms and a small bathroom. It was beautifully simple, the kind of house I'd dreamed of running away to when life – even Daniel – got to be too much. No TV, no computer; just books, a fireplace, a kitchen, and a bed. It was missing only one thing...that's when I turned around and found her: Jet, my black Labrador from my childhood. She trotted up and put her nose into my hand. I went to the kitchen to put a kettle on for tea and stepped back outside to inspect the greenhouse.

It was empty of all plants except for the oak bonsai. Its perfection was no longer apparent – some of the wiring work I had done hadn't taken and it stuck out in odd angles. Roots strained out of the water holes in the bottom, begging for pruning and repotting. I finally smiled at this imperfection and resolved to take care of it. After the tea. And after fetch with Jet.

My euphoria had lifted, but I was thankful for this. I felt a little like myself again. I was sad about losing Daniel, but not as if we'd broken up. It was kind of like putting down a bag of potato chips when you knew they were empty calories, no matter how good they tasted. My new resolve was to succeed alone. I smiled when I realized I'd taken the hard way. I decided to tell Grandma Melissa if I ever saw her again. The real her, of course.

Certainly, a small part of me still pined for Daniel, but that feeling had been ever-present since eighth grade, and was something I could ignore when I had to. I was good at it.

A solitary existence, complete with imperfections, might be hard at first,   but   at   least   it   was   honest.

CHAPTER FIVE

I grew to learn time means nothing in heaven. I still received newspapers on occasion, any time I ever wondered about earth or people I had loved. I did remember to check up on my parents, and actually mourned the relationship we'd never had. I'd never been the perfect girl they had wanted; I suppose their perfection seemed so false that I took it as hypocrisy, and ran fast and hard the other way.

It was clear from my checkups that they were spiraling downhill, the dual stress of losing me and Grandma Melissa driving them apart. You'd hope that such shock would have made them treasure each other more, but Mom had taken up scrapbooking on all her free time, and Dad seemed on a fast track to a heart attack. He'd put on at least thirty pounds and generally lived in filth, beer cans piling up around him in the den. Neither of them cleaned. I realized with sadness that I might be seeing him in heaven sooner rather than later.

I missed the handful of friends from the flower shop and the college friends who'd stayed in the area, but I knew I'd eventually see them all at one point or another. I honestly wished them long lives; I had eternity to wait, after all.

I didn't receive reports that any other relatives had died, but I didn't trust to ever see the real people if they died anyway; most of us weren't that close. Solitude had never been something I had enjoyed while living, but I realized that back then I had been afraid of it. Being alone wasn't so bad. Besides, it was better to make the active choice to be alone than to spend your whole afterlife afraid of it. I was never bored: I tended my garden, I played with Jet, and I read countless books and newspapers. My afterlife took on an air of silent contentment.

I didn't know if Jet was real or not, but I figured she was. Dogs loved unconditionally, so it would make sense that she would want to be with me. Then again, I remembered that my Sunday school teacher from my youth said that dogs didn't have souls. Who knew? I didn't care, honestly, and didn't want more horrible truths handed to me by the almighty God.

My repotted oak tree survived, although it never was the spitting image of perfection. I loved it for that reason alone - I often felt like it and Jet were the only genuine things around me. I kept it in the greenhouse, but pulled it out on occasion to get some fresh air and light – or, to be honest, to give me a dose of reality.

Loneliness wasn't an issue. At least, I thought it wasn't until one day there came a knock at the door.

I raced to get it, Jet barking up a storm behind me. Suddenly thrilled at the prospect of seeing another face, any face, I opened the door.

Daniel stood on my front porch, smiling ruefully. "Kate? Is it really you?"

#

I made him tea. He turned it down. This comforted me; the Daniel I knew had always hated tea.

"So, tell me about your heaven," I said when we'd settled.

"When I first got to heaven there were, well, a lot of women waiting for me. I spent most of my time with them...at least at first."

I snorted to hide my disappointment. "I didn't know you were a Muslim."

He glared at me. "It didn't last the whole time. I fell for one of them, Miranda, and we were married. We opened up a soup kitchen downtown."

"There's a downtown in heaven? There are *homeless* in heaven?"

He nodded. "That's when I realized there was something wrong. In paradise, there's no one to help. Then heaven created some happy homeless people for me to help. It was hollow.

"Once I figured this out, I talked to Miranda to find out about her life on earth. She spun some story that didn't really work out. It was pretty confusing; here was my dream girl, smart, funny, and sexy as hell, but I couldn't get a handle on where she came from, you know? Who she really was. Then God showed up and we talked."

I rubbed my arms. "Yeah, pretty much the same thing on my end."

"Really? What was your heaven before this?"

I tried to form a lie and then felt self-conscious about committing a flagrant sin (but then again, he said he had been able to have lots of premarital sex in Heaven, so what did that mean?).

"Eh, it's not something I'm ready to talk about yet," I managed to say. "But I figured it out like you did, and then ended up here. Before you, the last person I saw was God."

"Living alone is the last place I'd expect you to be," he said.

I shrugged and didn't meet his eyes. "It was better than the alternative. And it's been fun. Or at least real."

"Pretty fucked up, huh?" he said, frowning at his hands. Apparently swearing was cool in heaven, too.

"So what happened after you talked to God?"

"For one thing, I felt like my head was clear for the first time since getting here. And I wondered where you were. So I started walking, going mostly on instinct, till I finally landed here."

I smiled. Tears threatened to overtake my resolve, so I got up to stoke the fire and hastily wipe my eyes.

"So now that you're here, what now? Wanna be roommates? I've got a small house, but I'm sure adding a room won't be a problem. This place is pretty easy to manipulate when you want something."

He didn't answer. When I looked up from the fireplace he was looking out my window at the road.

"Remember when we said we'd take a trip out west if we had enough money, during Spring Break?"

"Sure," I said, feeling a blush rise to my cheeks. I had hoped and fantasized that it would be a trip full of epic, movie-worthy romance, all the while knowing, of course, that it would be like every moment with Daniel: fun, spontaneous, and devoid of anything deeper.

"Well, why don't we do something like that now? I think we should explore."

I cupped my mug and sat down on my sofa. "If everything here is fabricated, to make us happy, what's the fun in exploring? Besides that, where would we go?"

He met my eyes. "I don't mean in this heaven. When I talked to God, I asked Him why He was a bearded English-speaking white guy. Turns out, he's black to the blacks and Italian to the Italians. When I asked him about whether the Christians were right and everyone else was in hell, he said that everyone had their own heaven. Or hell. I think we can get to those places. What do you think? Want to try?"

I blinked at him, feeling stupid for not having asked myself the same thing. "Uh, well, even if we could explore them, how would we get in? We might have been good enough to get into Christian heaven, but I'm pretty sure we don't qualify as Jews, Muslims, or Buddhists, just to name a few."

He opened his backpack and pulled something out a velvet ring box. My face flushed, but he looked more pleased with himself than he did a man in love, so I willed my hands not to shake as I took it. Inside was not a ring after all, but a necklace; a gold chain holding a diamond cross. It was heavy and gaudy, the diamonds sparkling brightly whenever they caught the light. I looked up at Daniel, trying to smile.

He snorted. "Don't look at me that way. I know it's awful, but look." He pulled one out of his own shirt and held it to the light. "Jewish," he said. The diamonds moved to form a Star of David. "Wiccan," he said, and it became a five-pointed star. He went through a couple more religions, and the diamonds always formed their signature symbols.

"That's great, Daniel, but what does it mean? I doubt it takes a necklace to get into heaven these days. I know I wasn't wearing a cross."

"It's a passport, Kate! It marks us as travelers through the afterlife."

I finally took mine out and peered at it. "How did you get this? Cracker Jack box? Happy Meal? God doesn't just give them out, does He?"

Daniel stashed his necklace under his shirt. "He said He gives them only to travelers. Some people arrive here and are happy with paradise. They feel this is their reward for a life well lived. But some people aren't done with their journey. They have more traveling to do. So He sends them on a kind of walkabout to wander the afterlives. Sometimes He has jobs for them to do, He said, but I don't think that's us."

I stared at the pendant for a moment. I was happy here in heaven, in my solitary bungalow with my dog and my real plant. Daniel didn't love me; that was obvious by the description of his heaven. But eventually he had sought *me* out. That meant something. It meant more than most of the things that had happened since my death.

I slipped the necklace over my head and inside my shirt. "So, how does one pack for a trip through the afterlife?" I asked.

In the end, we packed some books on world religions and history, the special fuzzy socks that I liked to wear at night, a notebook, and my teapot. When we were done, I looked around my little house. It was time to go. Jet wagged her tail by the door. "Jet wants to go, too." "I don't see why not, unless she's not real," Daniel said.

"I think she is," I said. "I guess we'll find out."

CHAPTER SIX

To my surprise, once we left the pearly (wrought iron) gates, the road was unlike the one I had walked on my way to heaven – or I suppose I should start calling it Christian heaven. The sky was a clear blue, not the grayish white blandness I remembered, and the road was a white asphalt with golden arrows pointing back toward heaven. We ignored them.

After walking that road for some time, we approached a massive roundabout with dozens of roads branching out from it like spokes, each stretching to the horizon. Each road was composed of a different material; one was made of packed dirt, another of small stones, and another of red clay. Wooden boards made up yet another, and another seemed to be made from woven reeds.

"Where do you want to go first?" I asked, turning in a circle. I tried to count the roads, but lost count after twenty or so.

"Dunno. Where do you want to go?" he asked, kicking a stone. It bounced across the road and into the center of the roundabout: a flawless bed of white sand. It rolled a couple of feet and came to rest at the edge of the circle.

I snorted. "This isn't dateless Saturday night, Daniel. You honestly have no idea where you want to go?"

I stepped into the sand bed, which was surprisingly firm, and crossed to the stone. It lay in front of a road lined with cobblestones. "How about this one?"

He shrugged. "Works for me."

I wondered how smart it was to wander blindly into an unknown heaven, but this was an adventure after all, so we headed forward with purpose. The white sky never changed, but after a while I began to wonder how long we had traveled. My feet felt fine, but mentally I began to drag. I nearly wept with relief when Daniel suggested we stop.

"Look, clearly there's no night here, but I'm getting sick of this scenery," he said, stamping down a circle in the tall grass beside the road. The road had become hilly; the drab landscape had gained grass, but not much else.

"Or lack thereof," I said.

He pulled some granola bars from his backpack and passed me one. I tore into mine, but he held onto his. "So where do you think this one goes?"

"Dunno," I said, my mouth full. I was suddenly ravenous, eyeing his unopened bar.

"Don't you think we should be prepared?"

"Well, we've got this lovely white-guy bling that's supposed to keep us safe, right?"

He shook his head. "First, don't say 'bling.' You sound like a moron. Secondly, that's the thing. I don't think they're supposed to keep us safe; they're just our passport into the heaven. What happens after that is up to us."

I swallowed. "So we're just wandering around without map or any means of protecting ourselves?"

"Pretty much. But it's not as if we could have gone down to the heaven Walmart and purchased guns before we left. I'm pretty sure there aren't guns in heaven. Or Walmart, now that I think about it. And if there are Walmart guns, the waiting list has got to be a bitch."

"We can't be killed, can we? I mean, we already did that."

"I don't think so, but…" he reached out and pinched me. I slapped his hand away. "People can hurt us. Or lock us up."

"You're just a bucket of sunshine, aren't you?" I tried to keep my tone light.

"Just thinking out loud. Wondering if we should stock up on, I dunno, afterlife mace or something."

I laughed. "I'll let you know if I find any, and then I'll pick up two."

He grinned at me. "So, do you think we can go to hell?"

I shook my head. "I don't know, but would you really want to? I think hell is a lot like pirates."

He stared at me with so much confusion that I laughed. "I mean that they're both shown in movies and stuff as funny things. Pirates versus ninjas, pirates versus zombies. It's all fun. But pirates were terrible people - murderers, rapists, thieves - and they probably smelled really bad. Hell is always a place with fire, but no one gets burned, and it's full of tax collectors and demons that are easy to outwit. I don't think hell is really a place we would want to visit. Especially if you're right about this necklace not being able to keep us safe. Imprisoned in, say, the pagan heaven would be different than being imprisoned in hell. Just my guess."

"I guess you're right."

We took some water from a canteen and passed it between us, pouring about half into a bowl for Jet. She lapped it up, spraying more water around than actually getting any in her mouth.

"So I never found out," Daniel said. "What really made you go to the homeless shelter that night? Why does your grandma of all people think you're a coward? I thought she was pretty cool."

I wiped water from my lips. "Why do you ask?"

He looked down at the flattened grass and pulled at a stalk. It stood up, looking alone and out of place. "I've been feeling sort of guilty. If I hadn't bullied you into going, you wouldn't be dead."

I lay back on my elbows and looked at the sky. "I just figured it was time to actually do something. I took the easy way out too often. That's why Grandma called me a coward."

He stared at me. "I'm sorry."

"Why? I'm not."

He looked at the lonely stalk of grass. "Are you ready to go?"

I nodded.

We stood up and started walking up the next hill. As soon as we crested it, the scenery finally changed. The tall grass remained, but a forest of dark trees dotted the horizon to our left, while fruit trees had appeared at the tops of the hills. Springs bubbled into stone fountains; some fresh water, some a bloody-looking liquid. A shallow clear stream cut through one of the hills and stretched to our right towards a glittering expanse that looked to be a sea.

But the best part was the people. Finally, we got a glimpse of someone else who wasn't fabricated to populate our heaven. I looked at Daniel and grinned, convinced that this journey had been a good idea.

People milled around, dressed in togas and robes, sitting under trees, reading books, or napping. Ahead, the road bisected a grand market and ended at what looked like a coliseum.

"Where are we?" Daniel whispered.

Before I could answer, a voice spoke up from behind me, "Elysium."

We hadn't heard her approach us, but I gasped audibly when I saw the speaker. I am petite and thus always envied women with height and strength. The woman behind us stood six feet tall at least, with a slender but well-muscled frame. She grinned at us, a lock of red-gold hair falling into her face. She wore a short toga and a belt from which hung three golden apples.

When I was a little kid, I had loved reading about the Greek myths. One of my favorites had been a kid-friendly book that used the word "married" instead of "raped," taking a lot of the horrific parts out of the stories and just making them about a lot of powerful gods running around and having fun. When I was a senior, I felt rather naive when I read the myths the way they were meant to be told, but I still loved the ones that were less personally violating and more heroic.

"Elysium, that's Greek, right?" Daniel said, watching three laughing women dip goblets into a fountain of red wine.

"Elysium is where the heroes go after death," the woman said. She gave our twenty-first-century clothes an appraising look. "Are you Travelers?"

We nodded and brought out our necklaces, which were now in the shape of lightning bolts.

"You'll want to see the games, then. But first, try the market; it's glorious. Enjoy, friends. I hope to see you again." She shifted a bow strung across her back and dashed down the road.

"Wow," Daniel said, swallowing hard. I suppressed my annoyance. What was I supposed to feel? Shit, if it were a choice between that warrior woman and myself, I know whom I would choose.

"Yeah. That was Atalanta, I think."

"Who?"

"Hero. Abandoned because she wasn't a boy, brought up by wolves, grew up to be a mighty huntress. Helped kill the Calydonian Boar and won nearly every footrace she ran in. The only one she lost was the one where her opponent kept throwing golden apples off the course so she'd run after them."

"Huh. She must have wanted to lose," he said.

"That's one theory," I answered. Atalanta's red-gold braid bounced as she neared the market and she soon disappeared into the crowd.

"Sounds like you know a lot about this place," Daniel said, handing me a white robe from his backpack.

"Where'd you get this?" I asked.

Daniel pulled out a second robe. "The backpack. I felt it get heavier when we got to the top of the hill."

I slipped the robe over my head. "Nice! So, the Cliff Notes version of Elysium: most of the regular dead people go to the Underworld, ruled by Hades and Persephone, but the heroes come here. It's their paradise."

"So, like, we could run into Hercules?"

"Heracles," I corrected. "Hercules was his Roman name."

"Heracles. Sure. Any other faux pas I should watch out for?"

I snorted. "Yeah. Be very alarmed if someone wants to 'marry' you."

#

The market roared with activity; well-dressed people buying live geese, squid, olive oil, jars of spices, butchered lamb, bottles of wine, and escorts of both sexes, to name a few. Merchants called out their wares, birds flapped their wings in a panic when men on horses rode by, and everyone wore a smile.

Daniel and I had pulled our necklaces to the outside of our robes to show everyone the symbol of Zeus. Merchants greeted us with loud voices, showing us jewelry, food, rugs and pets. I purchased a length of silk to tie around Jet's neck just in case she ran off; I think I horrified the merchant, but he knew better than to speak up. In his eyes I was a wealthy dead hero – who was he to tell me what I should do with his fine silk?

The mysterious backpacks we carried seemed to have everything we needed, including money pouches.

"God told me that there is little use for money in any heaven, but people enjoy exchanges, so it's limitless," Daniel said.

The merchants seemed grateful for the gold and silver coins, and Daniel and I had fun shopping. I put some bottles of wine in the backpack and Jet cheerfully carried the large lamb bone I purchased for her. Daniel munched on a spiced sausage speared on a skewer. I had always wanted to travel, and this was better than any place I could have dreamed of visiting.

Although the merchants' stalls still buzzed with activity, traffic moved always down the street toward the coliseum. Daniel stopped a young boy with impossibly golden curls and blue eyes.

"Excuse me, when do the games start?"

The boy stared at him for a moment, then his eyes dropped to the necklace. He nodded once and said, "One hour, but you should go get a seat now. They only happen once every seven years." "Wow, we're in luck," Daniel said to me.

The boy scampered off before Daniel could ask anything else. The crowd had begun to drift toward the coliseum, so we followed the other merrymakers, many of them drunk, into the gargantuan stone building. I shivered as we entered the marble staircase and thought of my grandfather's tomb in a marble mausoleum, complete with dank air and UV bug zapper. People seemed to be sitting where they liked, so we scouted a spot on some velvet-covered stone benches at the front.

I tried to see where people would be entering the sandy field to compete, but just as I was looking around, a lightning bolt cracked down and hit the center of the field, blinding me. Daniel and I were the only ones to flinch and cover our ears as a response to the flash and thunder; everyone else applauded. When my eyes had re-adjusted to the light of the day, I grabbed Daniel's arm and pointed.

The massive gods – they could have been no one else – sat upon thrones of gold across the coliseum from us, looking down at the field and around at the audience.

"Jesus, even I know who those people are," Daniel whispered. We applauded along with the rest. Zeus and Hera occupied the center two thrones, Zeus openly grinning through his beard and Hera's cold eyes searching the stands. Dragging my eyes from the king and queen of the gods, I searched for my favorite heroes of my childhood.

Athena was not dressed in her warrior's garb, but I knew immediately it was her; she whispered to an owl that sat on her shoulders, and her face was serene and intelligent.

Artemis, Hermes, and Hephaestus were all there, Hermes grinning wryly at something the bulky, heavy lidded Ares was saying, and Hephaestus glaring at the same. Artemis sat beside her twin, Apollo, both of them wearing bows strung across their backs. All of the others were there as well: Poseidon with his trident, Demeter,

Dionysus, and Aphrodite, whose beauty tended to drag my eyes to her, even though she was not my favorite by a long shot.

I pointed out who was who to Daniel, who seemed to only want to know about Aphrodite. I tried to tell him that anyone who tried to sleep with her would piss off not only her husband, Hephaestus, but her lover, Ares, the god of war. He shrugged off my concern and said there was no crime against looking. I thought of the myth about the poor bastard who accidentally stumbled across Artemis bathing in the woods and was turned into a stag for his transgression, which really was only that of being at the wrong place at the wrong time. He had been torn apart by his own hounds. I gulped.

Not that the gods weren't distracting me from my concern (all right, it was *jealousy*) over Daniel's divinely-inspired crush. Throughout my childhood I'd always loved Hermes, the runt, the manipulator, who had tricked Apollo out of an entire herd of cattle when he was only a day old. The god's dark curls fell into his eyes as he looked my way and I felt my insides clench and my face get hot. *Oh, great.*

No one announced anything, but a trumpet sounded and doors opened at either end of the coliseum. From one end, two tigers ran onto the sand, snarling with their ears back. They bled from wounds on their backs; someone had wanted them quite angry upon entering the arena.

From the other entrance came a man and woman, confident and proud. He carried a sword; she, a bow and spear.

"Hey, it's Atlanta!" yelled Daniel amidst the cheers.

"Atalanta," I corrected. I looked at the grand cats and then at the warriors and bile clogged my throat. I don't like blood. I cursed myself;

what the hell had I been expecting, a chess game? But still, this was amazing.

A goddess, Artemis, stood up from the dais. She raised her hand and the crowd fell silent. I could not *believe* I was sitting here watching Greek gods and heroes. The afterlife was so cool.

"Welcome, friends. Our traditional seven-year games begin with a traditional hunt. Our heroes are Heracles..." The crowd screamed its approval. "...and Atalanta." More cheers as the woman waved to her supporters.

I tore my eyes from the glorious woman to the man. Impossibly muscled, Heracles wore nothing but his lion skin cape. Dark streaks covered his body, and I realized it was centaur blood. Heracles had smeared the blood of his wife's kidnapper on himself, thinking it would make him stronger, but instead it caused him such pain that it nearly killed him. Zeus had brought him bodily to Elysium to end his suffering.

Daniel whistled at Heracles's nakedness. "Dude, one of the first things I would do if I were facing tigers is protect my junk." I laughed. "Hey, you know how cats like to play with dangly things!"

Atalanta hadn't been as bold (or as stupid). Fully clothed in a leather breastplate which covered her toga, she hefted her spear, testing its weight and firming her grip. She bowed to her goddess, Artemis, who remained unsmiling. Heracles also bowed.

"The first to bring a tiger down is the winner. If one manages to bring them both down, then he or she will be crowned champion." The crowd roared again and the heroes moved forward. The hunt was on.

"Isn't this like shooting fish in a barrel?" Daniel asked. "I mean, two legendary heroes and two cats in an enclosed space without trees?

Oh. Wait."

Heracles had had the same thought as Daniel and was taking the direct route. He charged the tigers, roaring louder than his prey. As he raised his sword, the tiger suddenly winked out of sight and reappeared, looking slightly alarmed, in the middle of the arena.

Heracles was no fool. He looked up at the gods balefully. Athena hid a smile in her owl's feathers. Ares scowled at her.

Atalanta watched all of this carefully. As she lifted her spear and heaved it across the sand, I gasped at her strength. Before the spear reached her target, however, this tiger also disappeared and reappeared in the middle. She nodded slowly and unstrung her bow. She didn't look up at the gods, but I did, and caught Ares grinning triumphantly at Athena, who rolled her eyes.

Heracles dashed to the other end of the arena, swiping at one disappearing tiger and then the other. "Not too bright, is he?" I said. Daniel laughed. The tigers ended up at the original end of the area again, where Atalanta had been aiming. She immediately let fly her arrows-two from the bow at once!-and skewered both before Ares could interfere. Both tigers fell, arrows through their right eyes, and Atalanta grinned in triumph.

The crowd screamed their approval and the gods clapped politely, for the most part. Ares snarled and Hermes looked bored, his blue eyes skimming the crowd, seeming to rest on Daniel and me, and then moving on.

Atalanta waved at the crowd, blowing kisses and walking the perimeter of the arena. As she passed us, I cheered and clapped till my hands hurt.

She was focusing on the crowd and therefore didn't see Heracles's rage as he simmered, red-faced, in the center of the arena. I thought he must be screaming, but the noise of the crowd drowned everything out. The failed hero set off toward Atalanta with his sword raised. She didn't turn; she was busy still waving at her admirers.

"Atalanta!" I screamed, but I could barely hear myself - there was no way she was going to hear me. The crowd's tone had changed, but they still screamed and Atalanta didn't notice the change. The gods watched with detached interest.

I looked around. Wasn't anyone going to do something?

There are times in your life where shock paralyzes you. When you look up and see the softball coming toward your face and you know you can either put out your glove and catch it or move out of the way and let it whoosh past; but you don't. You just let it smack you in the face.

There are other times in your life where shock moves you as if you were controlled by an outside remote; you move, act, and speak without thinking. When it's all over with, you wonder how the hell you did it.

Shock is the easy way out. Waiting for someone else to act was the easy way out. Daniel and I stood together; he had a determined look on his face that I'll never forget. Then we vaulted over the railing to drop the eight-or-so feet into the arena's sand and took off for Atalanta ourselves, shouting her name, with one of the greatest heroes of legend bearing down on us.

CHAPTER SEVEN

The funny thing is that as we ran, Heracles covering about three yards for every one of ours, I found myself praying. I wasn't sure to whom, as we were already surrounded by gods. Would they listen?

Please, I thought. Nothing else; just, *please..* I forgot that I was here because of direct intercession from God, or that deities surrounded me. I just hoped, because I sure as hell didn't have a plan. It looked as if Daniel and I would soon find out whether we could die in heaven or not.

Heracles, luckily, had much more ground to cover than we did. Only seconds had passed since Daniel and I had decided to turn into heroes. The crowd continued to scream, and the gods watched us impassively. I saw Hermes reach out to Athena, but had to return my focus to the issue at hand. Atalanta took notice of us at last, frowning, and I pointed behind her.

She turned; Daniel reached her right before I did and stepped in front of her. Heracles was only ten feet away, now pounding down upon them. Atalanta's spear was still stuck in the sand at the other end of the arena and she had just strung her bow across her shoulder. We had nothing to attack or defend ourselves with.

So my thoughts went for the next best thing: dirty tricks.

I dove in front of Daniel and rolled, my momentum taking me toward Heracles's feet, straight on. His foot caught my belly and he tripped, and the air left my lungs in a great whoosh. A rib cracked and I curled up on my side, not focused on anything except the attempt to coax air back in. Heracles's fall caused a great wave of sand to spray over me, blinding me. Deafened as well by the crowd, I had no idea what was going on.

My diaphragm finally stopped spasming and I breathed deeply, wiped my eyes, and sat up. Expecting to see Atalanta's and Daniel's bodies soaking the sand with their blood, I braced myself, but what was before me made me gasp. Heracles was still prone on the sand with the goddess Athena standing with one sandaled foot on his sword wrist. Atalanta held Athena's mighty shield - acquired how and when I didn't know – in front of her and Daniel. Hermes stood beside his sister and bound Heracles's feet with a wave of his hand. The crowd finally stopped cheering, and a confused silence surrounded us.

Ares appeared next to his kin. "You had no right to interfere!" he barked at Athena. His voice surprised me; it was small and high and reminded me of Mike Tyson.

"He had lost, Ares," Athena said. "And he was unsportsmanlike. That is not the spirit of the games."

"The rules are no interference!" he said.

"More rules than that were broken," she snapped.

Artemis appeared and everyone appealed to her. Obviously the sponsor of these games, she turned and made a gesture to her father, Zeus. He raised his arm and my world filled with light. I must have passed out before the thunderclap came.

#

Cold seeped through my clothes, and as Daniel shook me gently awake, I realized we were on a marble floor somewhere damp. Loud voices argued from the next room. I shivered.

"What happened?"

"It sounds like the gods are arguing about the winner. They're trying to figure out if Athena and Hermes interfered and made the match forfeit."

"Kinda like when the marching band goes on the field before the football game is over?" I asked, rubbing my eyes.

"Something like that, yeah."

"So have they figured out why the gods interfered? I figured Athena helped us out because she's all about fair play, but why was Hermes there? He's the opposite, you'd think he'd like dirty tricks. That's his thing."

"You're the expert. I just know suddenly they were there handing over that shield and Atalanta used to it to keep that linebacker-gonemad from hamstringing us. Quick thinking, though, in tripping him. I didn't have a plan."

I sat up straighter and gasped as my rib let me know it wasn't very happy. I pressed on it with my hand. "I didn't have much of one either. Man, they're really yelling. I guess it's a big deal. So they don't care that he was trying to kill her?"

Daniel helped me to my feet. "They're more concerned with whether it was unsportsmanlike instead of deadly. I'm still not sure if you can die here. Hey, are you okay?"

I panted shallowly, not wanting to expand my chest. "I think Heracles cracked my rib. Maybe broke it. I'm not sure."

"Oh man. I guess we can be hurt, then."

"No shit," I said. I brushed the sand off me. Clouds floated by the open windows of the sparse marble hallway, and I looked out. "Shit, Daniel. Where's the ground?"

"I think we're in Olympus. Isn't that at the top of a mountain or something?"

I nodded, remembering. The shouting gods got louder. "Let's see what all the fuss is. But remember, they're gods. Do that, 'don't speak till spoken to' thing, because they're good at tricking humans. Especially Aphrodite."

"Is that the hot one?"

I groaned. "Just come on."

We peeked around the open door. Most of the gods sat on their grand thrones made of gold and silver, Zeus and Hera in the center. Athena and Hermes stood before the thrones by Atalanta on the left, with Ares and Aphrodite on the right with Heracles. Both heroes stood proudly, although disarmed.

Artemis stood. "The match was over. I rule his actions were reprehensible and illegal, and therefore my siblings did not interfere."

Aphrodite pouted, her breasts straining at the thin material barely containing them. Long strands of blonde hair curled gently over her chest, one lock delicately circling the distinct rosy impression of a nipple. I poked Daniel to keep him from staring. "Father, how can you let Artemis take the responsibility of the games if she is going to rule poorly?"

A god with a great beard tangled with seaweed stood from his seat on Zeus's left. I guessed it was Poseidon, god of the sea. "Your father determined she was the games sponsor. Do you doubt his judgment?" He walked slowly, with purpose, to stand by Atalanta.

Zeus watched him. His voice, unlike Ares's, was exactly as I expected it to be: deep, powerful, and commanding. "Is that how it will be, my sisters and brothers? Sons and daughters? Shall we choose sides?"

Dionysus stood. I guessed it was the god of wine because he wavered and blinked drunkenly like my uncle Casey at Christmas.

"The party is never over when you think it will be," he said, and joined Heracles.

"What does that even mean?" Daniel whispered to me. I shushed him.

Apollo joined Atalanta, siding with Artemis, his twin. Hephaestus limped, frowning bitterly, to stand by Aphrodite, despite the fact that his wife had eyes only for Ares. Demeter, eyes downcast and mumbling something about what was fair, joined Heracles. Artemis, having already stated her case, joined Atalanta.

Zeus and Hera remained. When the king of the gods focused on me, I felt it: something electrical. "What of the two humans? What is their role?"

We walked forward, unbidden but utterly sure that we were expected to. Daniel spoke first.

"We saw Heracles attack Atalanta after the match was over. She couldn't hear it when we yelled to look out, so we went to, uh, help."

"And you thought you could do what?" Hera asked, her cold eyes on me.

"I – I'm not sure. Warn her, I guess."

"But you didn't. You interfered well before any god did."

"There's nothing in the rules about that," Artemis said. "We just never expected someone to jump into an arena with tigers and heroes." She looked at us as if we were annoying bugs she'd found in her pillow.

"They are the true criminals here!" Ares shouted. "Only with their sacrifice will I be satisfied."

Hermes reached out and took my arm, pulling me close. He reached at my neck and pulled at the chain, his fingers stroking my collarbone. My breath quickened at the look in his merry eyes. He was a *god.*

Hermes held up the symbol on my necklace to Zeus. "They are Travelers, Father, and under my protection."

I wanted to smack my forehead. Hermes was the god of travel; of course he would have an interest in us.

"I demand their sacrifice!" Ares shouted again. Sure, he was the god of war, but I still wondered what Aphrodite saw in him.

"No," Hermes said, his arm still on mine. I was dizzy with his scent. Daniel shot me a curious look.

Ares put his hand on the great sword at his side. "Are you going to stop me, little brother?"

Hermes just grinned.

"He can't, but I can," Athena interrupted, her hand on her own sword. Poseidon stepped up, gripping his great trident, and the tension in the room rose dramatically. Hephaestus, with a furtive glance at his wife, stepped forward holding his blacksmith's hammer. Not much of a weapon, really, but I didn't want to feel it embedded in my skull.

"Now, wait a minute," Daniel said, but Zeus interrupted him.

"I do not want my children fighting," he said, the sorrow in his voice not very convincing. His voice had an edge to it, and although my proximity to Hermes was distracting me, I still felt adrenaline rush to my limbs when he spoke, my body telling me to run far, far away.

The gods began arguing loudly, and even Heracles and Atalanta, the legends, shrank back at the heat that rose in the throne room. Hermes pulled me back and I grabbed Daniel to go with us, out of the tense crowd of gods, now hurling insults with Athena and her sword between Ares and us. Once we were free of the other divine eyes, we... weren't there anymore.

The antechamber in Olympus went back, and then the whole of Elysium appeared, seen from the crest of the hill. I felt dizzy with the sudden change and leaned briefly against Hermes.

"Whoa," Daniel said, staggering.

Hermes let go of me and stepped back, appraising me. He then looked up into the sky where Olympus hung in the clouds over Elysium. Lightning cracked, and the clouds gathered, getting blacker.

"It looks like you Travelers have actually succeeded in splitting Olympus," he said, sounding more impressed than angry.

"Wait, what?" I asked, rubbing my eyes and trying to will away the dizziness. "The gods have fought in the past, haven't they?"

"Yes, but never have we split equally. If Zeus chooses one side and Hera the other, then that will start a war."

"But that's stupid!" Daniel said. "It was just one dirty trick during a game! Worse things have happened in history! Shit, athletes back home broke the rules all the time!"

"And were the games sacred there?" Hermes said, glaring at us.

I paused. Important, yes. Lots of attention, sure. Sacred?

"Not much is truly sacred where you come from, is it?" Hermes reached out and rubbed my shoulder. My throat closed and all I could do is shake my head.

"Um, Kate?" Daniel's eyes were fastened on the clouds. The sky was black, and as we watched, a lightning bolt snaked down and split Olympus in two. The great marble hall floated apart above us. "Oh man. That can't be good."

Hermes followed his gaze. "Zeus and Hera have disagreed, making the sides even. I was right. You two are the heralds for the end times."

"No way! We're just Travelers," I protested.

"And it is prophesied that Travelers would enter Elysium to be the catalyst to the final battle."

The rain cut off any argument we could have made – the deluge came sudden and cold. Elysium's denizens ran, screaming, looking for shelter. Of course, there was none. It was Heaven – what need did they have for shelter from bad weather?

Daniel frowned. "Is there anything we can do?"

Hermes shook his head, his blue eyes still on me.

Daniel put his hand on my arm. "Kate, we need to head out of here before things get really bad. Come on." I could barely hear him over the thunder.

Hermes held my other arm. "Please wait. Allow me an hour of your time," he whispered into my ear. "After one hour, I will return you unharmed to your friend. I swear on the River Styx." I blinked, and my knees nearly buckled.

Normally, I wouldn't go off with a strange guy. That's what I told myself, anyway. But swearing on that river was sacred, and it was the most holy oath a god could make.

"Go on. I'll catch up," I told Daniel. His jaw dropped and I managed a smile. "I promise. I'll be okay; Hermes will make sure I find you."

I didn't see the look on his face as we left, but I imagined he was pissed. The world blurred for a moment and the next thing I knew, Hermes held me in a cave, safe from the storm.

"Where—"I managed to say, my head reeling.

"This is the cave where I was born. We are safe here. I still come here for privacy on occasion."

"But there's a war out there. Aren't you supposed to be—"

"It can wait. You are a Traveler, you are one of mine." He smiled at me and stroked my unruly hair out of my face. I was suddenly aware that I had to have been filthy: covered in sand and wide-eyed from all the adrenaline rushes the day had served me.

He bent his head toward mine but before he could touch my lips, I jerked back out of instinct. Part of my mind was screaming that I was crazy, flinching back from an unbelievably sexy guy, but I had had an intense day and I wasn't sure I could take much more.

The sudden pain in my injured rib silenced my inner argument. I gasped, my hands moving automatically to the spot.

Hermes frowned. "You're hurt?"

"Heracles gives quite a kick," I mumbled, holding my side and grimacing.

His hands went to mine and gently pried them away. He lifted my robe, unperturbed at the very non-Greek jeans-and-T-shirt combo underneath, and told me to hold it up for him. I did so, hands shaking a bit. Then he carefully lifted my shirt to just below my breast.

"Is this the injured rib?" he asked, his finger delicately running along my side. A deep, healing warmth flowed through me, and I couldn't tell if he'd healed me or just removed the pain. I nodded, testing the rib with a deep breath. The bruising had radiated from the rib, however, and other ribs complained as my chest expanded. I winced.

"Ah, not all better yet," he said, and began tracing my ribs from the bottom up, leaving hot trails in his wake. He stopped right below my breast and hesitated.

"Do you know why I brought you here?"

"No," I said honestly. My voice shook.

"There is a light inside you. A power. You are a Traveler, but not like I have seen before. You shine like a pyre."

"Me? Why?" My conversation had to be utterly enthralling. But I did have the distraction of his fingertips moving beyond a healing capacity and into a realm I'd experienced before-I was no virgin-but never, ever on the level this god offered....

"I can't tell you why. I can only tell you that it is." He leaned in and touched his lips gently to my ribs, and I jumped; this time from being startled.

He held me to him firmly as his mouth explored my ribs and stomach, with me holding my robe up stupidly, quivering.

He finally stood up and looked at me. "Now do you know why I brought you here?"

"I think so," I whispered. "Are you injured anywhere else?" I shook my head.

"Good," he said, and kissed me gently. He held me up when my knees finally gave way, threading his hands through my tangled hair and kissing me harder.

My robe was gone. I wasn't sure where. My shirt and jeans followed it. His hands were insistent; they roamed over my back, lingering at my breasts, my face, my thighs. A part of me wondered what would happen if I protested. The rest of me laughed at that part; no one would protest this intoxicating pleasure.

He lay me down on a blanket and removed his own tunic. He knelt beside me, his fingertips lazily teasing my nipples. I reached out and traced the contours of his sleek body, his tight muscles.

My fingers stroked along one area that made him moan, and he grew hard under my hand.

He slid a finger inside me and I arched my back. "Not a virgin, then," he said.

"Is that a problem?" I asked.

He moved between my legs. "On the contrary. I like a woman who knows pleasure. It also gives me a challenge." He lowered his head to lick once, quickly, like a cat. I gasped. He smiled once more at me, and dove in to feast.

The next hour was a blur. I know I came quickly, first from his mouth, and then he slowed and began a more leisurely exploration of my body. We tried several positions, each one better than the last, each time blowing my mind, making me drunk on pleasure.

At some point I think he changed his shape. Or maybe mine. Or both. I wasn't sure.

When he came, from behind me, he bit deeply into my shoulder, breaking my skin and marking me, the sudden sharp pain driving me over the edge again, leaving me sobbing and breathless.

#

I figured the cave would be chilly, after. But the proximity to Hermes made me warm. I lay on my stomach beside him, suddenly shy as he stroked his fingertips down my back.

"Why me?" I asked again.

"You honestly don't know?" His blue eyes twinkled under his black curls.

"Obviously not."

"Then I suppose it's something you should find out on your own, Kate. You have a long journey ahead of you. The answer will come to you."

I made a face, and he ran his thumb over my bottom lip. "I wish we had more time, my little Traveler. But it was a true pleasure to taste you on the cusp of everything."

I was about to ask, "The cusp?" but he kissed me again, and suddenly it didn't seem so important.

He deposited me at approximately the same area we had left, but Daniel was nowhere to be seen.

"You will find your friend down the road. He is walking slowly." Hermes pointed. "I would take you to him myself, but he has left Elysium and it would take me too long to get there. And, well..." he shrugged and pointed toward the sky where the storm continued to rage.

Armies of heroes, gods, and strange monsters gathered in the sky. The gods were split: six on one side and five on the other, with hundreds of backup deities. "What's going to happen?" I asked. "Is this really our fault?"

"Consider yourself a catalyst to something that was... inevitable," he whispered, and bit my earlobe. I shivered.

"I must go. But you are marked as a Traveler, and I will be watching you. Your friend, too-though he's not as much fun to watch, truth be told."

I laughed. He bent and kissed me and I savored his taste. Then he was gone in a flash of light.

My mind finally cleared and I swore silently to myself. I hit the road at a jog through the rain to catch Daniel and escape the battle that brewed. I didn't look back.

#

Daniel waited for me at the roundabout, sitting in the sand, glaring at me.

"What?" I said, trying to sound innocent.

"'What?' What do you think?" His voice became a bad highpitched imitation of mine. "'Watch out for Aphrodite, Daniel, she'll seduce you and piss the other gods off; quit looking at Atalanta, Daniel...' I turn my back for one second and you're going off with the first god that makes eyes at you! How mad would you have been if I'd gone off to sleep with one of the goddesses?"

I thought about it. I would have been utterly crushed, of course, but I wasn't going to tell him that. "I would have been pissed, true. But tell me this. If a goddess had presented herself to you, what would you have done? Honestly?"

He glared at me more, and I saw a smile twitch on his face. Finally he broke the tension by laughing. "All right. I would have gone for it. You got me."

"You're just mad because I got some divine tail and you didn't."

He shook his head at the ground and smiled, then stood and brushed the sand off his jeans. "So, it seems we've started a divine war in one heaven. Where to next?"

"Probably somewhere where we don't get into as much trouble," I said.

"Would you have done anything different, Kate? I mean, you got lucky with a *god*. When was the last time you had any, anyway?"

I looked at him and remembered having sex with his doppelganger in Heaven, but couldn't really remember what it was like. "I don't remember," I answered semi-truthfully.

"Then look at it this way," he said, slinging a companionable arm around my shoulders. "You're like that Helen chick – you got some and then a war started. And the best part? You got to leave without anyone laying claim to you."

I had nothing else to do but laugh. Without much consideration, we picked a road and set off toward another heaven.

#

"I can't believe we really caused all that." Daniel said after we'd wandered for some time.

I was still thinking of Hermes and worrying if I could get pregnant even though I was dead. I hadn't had my period since dying, and the time spent with the faux-Daniel seemed to indicate not, so I didn't think so, but the fear of pregnancy was a companion worry with sex. "Caused what?"

"That big war. Hermes called it the end days, the final battle. I just thought we were helping out someone who was about to be unfairly filleted."

I shrugged. "Hermes told me we were a catalyst to the inevitable. If we hadn't done it, someone else would have."

"That's not too heartening," Daniel said.

I thought about it. "I guess the thought of a bunch of gods that no one cares about anymore and a bunch of dead heroes having a final battle wouldn't have much impact anywhere else."

"And yet you were quite eager to help out one of those dead heroes."

"Well, if you're worried, what can we do about it?"

"I don't know. What do you say when you start an avalanche? 'Sorry!'"

I snickered. "Good point. Well, let's try not to do it again; will that make you feel better?"

He shrugged and squinted ahead. "I'm beat. Let's take a rest. You might want to call Jet back."

Jet, who'd apparently pranced around Elysium while Daniel and I had had our adventures, had been leading the way into this heaven, sometimes running far ahead, then bounding back and barking at us, then running ahead again.

"Well, we could rest for the night. If there were a night here," I said, looking at the gray sky.

"We got sleeping bags in these backpacks?" Daniel asked, pulling his off his back. I followed suit; mine held a poufy sleeping bag with Hello Kitty on it – Daniel snorted when he saw it – and a soft doggy bed. Jet ran back to us and immediately climbed onto her bed, turned round three times and lay down, staring at me. I scratched her behind her ears, and then she put her head on her paws and continued to watch me.

Although the sky was still a uniform gray, I was exhausted. I shook off Daniel's offer of food and crawled inside my sleeping bag and drifted off.

What does one dream about in heaven? I honestly didn't remember a lot of my dreams; when I was in the Christian heaven I usually woke up feeling blissful, but now that I was out on the road, I would awaken feeling disoriented, with an odd sense of foreboding. I'd woken up like this a lot when I was in high school, and after about sixteen I'd finally convinced myself that I was not psychic, just a weird dreamer.

This time, I'd dreamed of Hermes, naturally; only it wasn't a sexual dream. He stood in the roundabout at the center of all the Heavens, frowning at me. His hair obscured his eyes and blood ran from a cut on his left cheek. He opened his mouth to speak, but I only heard the boom of thunder.

I woke up with a start, the damnable sky refusing to tell me how much time had passed. I rubbed my face and sighed, feeling worse than when I'd gone to sleep.

Lovely dream. I pulled a canteen out of my backpack and drank deeply. Jet and Daniel still slept, Jet's paws twitching and her lips occasionally pulling back. She yipped quietly and I smiled, remembering the chasing dreams she'd had when we were alive. I wasn't going to get any more sleep, that was for sure, so I got out of my sleeping bag and put on my shoes.

It took only twenty paces further into this Heaven before I noticed that the fields had a distinct grassy smell, as if the grass had just been cut. I inhaled deeply, catching a scent of something small, something twitchy, something delicious.

I nearly dropped to my knees to find the source of the scent before I realized what was going on. I opened my eyes, unaware that I'd closed them.

The whole world was gray; not just the sky. Gray and drab, almost not worth keeping my eyes open. I laughed out loud, and caught sight of something on a hill in front of me. The sight told me very little, but the smell on the air told me everything.

I ran back to camp and shook Daniel awake. Jet raised her head from her bed and stared at me, thumping her tail on the ground.

"What the hell did you wake me up for? Claudia was just about to —" he protested, and I forced myself not to look at his sleeping bag for any tale-tell signs of, well, Claudia's influence.

"I know where we are. I know what heaven we're in!" I said. I went to my things and started stuffing them into my backpack.

"Well, is it dangerous?" he asked, dropped his head back onto his sleeping bag. "Nope."

"Then it can wait." He rolled over.

I grabbed his shoulder and pulled him back toward me. "No, it can't. It's too cool."

"Tell me, then, and I'll decide whether to kick your ass."

"Dog   Heaven."

CHAPTER EIGHT

It didn't take much more to get Daniel out of his sleeping bag. Jet was already trotting ahead of us, completely at ease in an alien world.

"This is so not right," Daniel mumbled.

"Why? It's cool!" I said, trying to identify the dozen scents on the air. Each had a different signature, like a different color.

"Oh, it's cool, all right. But I have this incredible desire to sniff your ass."

I blushed, glad for the black and white world. I stuck out my hand and grabbed his, shaking it. "You already know me. You don't need to confirm it with my scent. I'm Kate, and have no desire to have your nose in my butt."

He laughed, but after I let him go he sidled a couple of steps away from me.

My blush intensified when I realized that I very likely smelled as if I'd just had sex, which I had. Where does one find a shower in Heaven?

The field stretched before us, much like Elysium had, but without the fountains and fruit trees. It looked like an unchanging landscape, but my nose told me otherwise. Dogs of all shapes-mutts, Great Danes, shi tzus, poodles and, of course, Labrador retrievers-bounded in the fields, barking loudly, sniffing and rolling. Jet dashed forward, pulling the silk from my hands. I let her go, watching the handmade leash wave back at me.

After a thought, I bounded after her. She was investigating everything, and I wanted to be with her since I could finally see out of her eyes. Or nose.

One area of the field was covered in foul scents-rotten meat, old fish, dog feces-that somehow, now, seemed oddly appealing. I followed Jet to this area and found carcasses in the grass. I managed to pull myself up, remembering my *Homo sapiens* status, and watched wistfully as she grabbed a decaying possum in her jaws, shook it hard, and tossed it into the air. She watched it land, and then dropped and rolled on it.

The desire to join her was overwhelming, so I decided to investigate the other areas instead. Dogs were everywhere, some pulling at a fresh cow carcass, which looked less disgusting and more delectable every minute. Others ran after balls that flew from unseen hands. Some simply dozed in the sun. I spied my first human sitting on the side of a sloping hill, rubbing a sheepdog's belly, and ran to greet her.

"I didn't think there would be other humans here," I said as a greeting, fighting the urge to sniff her nether regions.

She grinned up at me, flipping her dark braid off her shoulder and shaking my hand. "Of course. Who else would give the belly rubs?" More humans waved to me at that point, each with one hand in the air and one on a dog's belly.

"How do you get on here with just dogs?"

"It's wonderful," she said, her eyes misty. "All the dogs I ever had are here, and I'm able to make up the times that I didn't walk, feed, or play with them. I have their senses now. I can finally see the world as they did."

I wondered if this woman was serving out some kind of penance. I leaned forward to sniff the air around her and found nothing but sincerity. She was happy here.

"What brings you here? Your dog?" she asked.

I waved my hand in the direction of the area I'd begun to think of as Carcass Central. "She's over there. She came to us in the Christian heaven and we've been wandering around as Travelers since." I pulled the chain out of my shirt to reveal a running dog.

"'We'?" she asked.

"My friend Daniel. He's, well, I don't know where he is, but he's here somewhere."

She wrinkled her nose. "If he's not all over you, then he's doing his best to stay far away. You smell as if you're in heat."

I straightened from the belly I was rubbing, and another human ran in to take my place. "That's really rude. Do you always address people you meet like that?"

Some sort of hormone began flowing in the woman, wafting off her: adrenaline. "Society's rules are different here. You'll have to get used to it. Your secrets come out of your pores; you can't hide much.

"And if you think it was a good idea to leave an intact male alone in a dog Heaven, you're stupider than you look," she added.

If I backed down at this point, I'd give this woman Alpha status over me. But then, I had Daniel to consider.

"'Intact male?'" I asked.

"Not fixed. Still in complete ownership of his testicles. Able to reproduce. Very attractive to bitches." Her lip curled as she said it, the implied insult obvious.

I gasped, no longer caring about the alpha dominance games.

"Where are the bitches in heat?" I asked.

Smiling in her superiority, the woman pointed to the top of the hill, where I saw a lone figure standing.

"Daniel!" I yelled, breaking into a run. The figure dropped to his knees, and I pushed myself to run faster. A small, sarcastic voice in the back of my head said that if I saw him doing what I feared he would be doing, I would pretty much lose my unrequited love for him forever.

When I reached him, he was clothed, on his knees, his hands covering his face. Bitches surrounded him, sniffing at his underarms, crotch, and neck. They licked whatever skin they could find. He sobbed into his hands, too weak to remove himself from the situation, but strong enough to resist the next step.

I shooed them away (gently, it *was* Dog Heaven after all) as best I could and pulled him to his feet. He peered at me through his fingers and said, "Get me out of here. Please."

I dragged him away from the bitches, who whined and barked. But they were soon distracted by males, of which there seemed to be an unending number. One male came sniffing towards me and I bared my teeth and growled at him; he turned to find another female.

"I have to get out of here. I can't stand it." Daniel practically sobbed, leaning on my shoulder. "You don't know what it's like."

"I can guess," I said, pulling him faster. The scents were overwhelming now, mostly of Daniel: fear and desire and despair.

I dragged him past the sunny fields of dead carcasses and selfthrowing balls to what looked like the edge of heaven, with color gently bleeding back into the gray, then deposited him into the grass. "Is this far enough away?"

He nodded, watching me with red-rimmed eyes. "Are you going back?" I'd never heard such petulance in his voice, such need.

"Only to get Jet, and I'll be right back."

Jet wasn't in the Carcass Central, nor was she in the Belly Rub Bordello. I knew she wouldn't be on the Hill of Love, since I'd had her fixed. A particularly gruesome section of the field crawled with squirrels, rabbits, and chipmunks which the dogs raced after, always catching their prey and destroying it with a neat shake of the head... but Jet wasn't there either.

I finally found her in the sunny area, lying in a patch of sunlight perfectly round, like a spotlight. I put my hand gently on her head and said, "Girl, it's time to go."

She raised her head and thumped her tail once. She whined low in her throat, and I caught her emotions on the air. Sadness. Desire to stay. And love. Overwhelming love. We think we know how much our dogs love us, but it's nothing, *nothing* like reality. I sat down next to her and rubbed her belly, and the love and contentment came off her in waves. She was happy here. She belonged.

"I have to go, Jet. I might be able to be happy here, but I have to get Daniel out. He can't stay."

Jet rolled over and licked my hand once. I scratched her on the head behind her ears the way she liked. "Can I come visit?" She wagged her tail again, and stretched out in the sun.

"Good dog," I whispered.

When I saw Daniel waiting on me, I wiped my eyes hastily, but he just smiled his half-smile. "Where's Jet?"

"Staying. I'm wondering if we were just supposed to bring her here and that was our mission."

"Could be, who knows why we're doing this," he agreed, giving me a quick hug. "Thanks for getting me out of there."

I pulled back. I'd been too distracted when carting him away from his lady friends to notice, but this close it was clear. Loud and clear. The smell coming from him was sour and underhanded.

"You're... lying," I said.

"What?"

"Lying. About this traveling. Why we're doing it. We're not doing it to help people or deliver Jet to her Heaven or whatever. There's another reason."

Daniel's jaw dropped open and his face flushed. We were far enough out of dog Heaven for me to catch the color in his cheeks, but still close enough for me to smell the strong scent of panic rising from him.

"Why did you lie, Daniel? Why are we really here?"

He just stared at me.

My fists clenched. "Fine. Don't fucking tell me. But I'm not following you around anymore. I thought I could trust you.

"When I got to heaven, you want to know what happened? God sent me a fake you to hang around with, a perfect you who—" I still couldn't say it. Couldn't say, "Loved me."

"When I found out he was fake, I decided to live alone. I can do it again, Daniel. If you're lying to me, you're not the friend I had in life. You've been sarcastic and aloof, but I always knew I could trust you. Now I don't know."

He still looked dumbfounded as I passed him and trudged up the road. I held the tears back by force of will, but I stopped when he finally spoke.

"I was your Heaven?" was all he said.

I turned around and faced him, the tears breaking my voice. "You really are an idiot, Daniel. You've had my hormones and emotions as an open book for the past few hours and you didn't even see it. Smell it. Whatever. Why did I have to fall in love with a moron?"

I left him then, his face slack with shock, on the road leading from dog Heaven. I left the thing that loved me more than anything else in the world lying blissfully in a patch of sunshine, and I left the person I loved more than anything else in the world standing slack-jawed and stupid on the road.

#

The look on Daniel's face was nearly gratifying in its relief as he approached me at the roundabout. I sat cross-legged on the sand and waited for him, stony-faced.

He didn't say anything, just came and sat beside me.

I pointed down a narrow dirt path. "I'm pretty sure that's a path to reincarnation. Tell me everything, or I'm heading down there. I might be a bug or a dog or something, but it'll be better than following you around like a lovesick puppy when you don't even tell me what's going on."

I knew I was right about the path, just like I knew Daniel was lying. The certainty lay cold and unemotional in my chest, keeping me calm.

Daniel's voice was flat. He didn't look at me. "I don't think I ever told you this, but my sister Megan died when I was ten. She was four. When people find out, I usually tell them it was an accident or something. But it wasn't. My mother went insane and killed her. I walked in right when she lost it, and tried to stop her. That's how I got these." He pushed up his sleeves to show me the long scars on his forearms. He'd always told me they were from a boy scouting accident.

"When I got to Heaven, the first thing I did was look for Megan. I couldn't find her. I couldn't imagine a girl that young going to Hell, so I tracked down God and asked Him what was going on. He said that some souls had gone missing, and He needed someone to investigate why. I asked Him when I could leave."

He stopped. Although this was all new information for me, I waited. There was more; his face told me that much.

He sighed. "One of the reasons souls are going missing, He said, was that it's time for the end of the world." My mouth went dry. "So Hermes was right." Daniel nodded.

"And it's even bigger than he said. It's not just Greek." It wasn't a question.

He nodded again.

I rubbed my face, trying to disbelieve. "So we're supposed to find lost souls and... what?"

I'd never seen him so miserable. "Bring about the apocalypse," he said. He frowned deeply and I realized he was trying not to cry. "The way I understand it, the end is coming whether we do this or not. But we need to be there. To witness or... help... or something. There are reasons He didn't make clear to me. He just told me we had to find the souls."

"What if we refuse?"

"I can't. You can. I'm sorry I didn't give you that option from the beginning, but I can't. I have to find Megan. I'd always imagined her in Heaven, in some kind of little kid paradise, and the fact that she's not there is killing me. If it takes witnessing the final battle to bring her back, I'll do it."

I tried to be understanding, but logical. "Daniel, we're talking about the world here. The end of the world. Billions of people."

"It's going to happen anyway. And I have to look for her. Don't you understand?"

My mouth was dry. "So it's an inevitability? Destiny?"

"Yeah, that's what He said."

"So the world ends. Then what?"

"I don't know. We're already dead. It gets more populated up here? I don't know. But every religion has an end of the world myth, doesn't it?"

I nodded reluctantly.

"We're just the ones who get to be around when it happens," he said.

"Lucky us." I sighed and rubbed my face again, trying to rub away the tears and frustration from the past hour. "So, where to next?"

He ventured a look at me. "You're still coming with me?"

I nodded. "Daniel, I've always got your back. You just need to tell me what we're up against. Besides, I don't think we have much choice in the matter. Where to next?"

He pulled out a book in his backpack and flipped through it. "Well, what end of the world myths are there? Didn't the Norse have a big one?"

I blinked. "Ragnarök? You're not messing around."

"Would you prefer a more sedate end of the world myth? Everyone lying down and going to sleep, maybe?" he asked. "I can't think of any that predict that."

"Fair enough," I said, and got up.

"Hey, Kate," he said, grabbing my arm. "I'm sorry."

I looked down, embarrassed. "I know you are, Daniel. Just give me a little time, okay?"

He nodded.

One of the roads exiting the roundabout was made of choppy water, and a Viking skiff bobbed at the edge. We stepped aboard and let   the   current   take   us   away.

BOOK TWO: DANIEL

CHAPTER NINE

I moved to Tennessee when I was twelve. My father had transferred there, taking me with him after the incident with my mother. He felt that leaving the shadow of Boston and its prying newspapers would be the best thing for us. My dad kept me out of school for as long as he could, but as soon as I did return, the reporters followed, snapping pictures of me outside the school, shouting questions at my father, asking if my wounds had healed. They tried to depict me as a hero, but when my father wouldn't allow them any interviews, they didn't have a juicy enough story to continue the sensationalism. So they made stuff up.

Of course, they got all the details when I had my time on the stand, and the newspapers went wild again. After the trial, we moved, and they didn't follow. We settled in Tennessee, laid low, and Dad found me a good child psychologist. I entered middle school and was seated beside a girl named Kate.

She hated me at first sight.

#

One thing He told me was that I would go where I was meant to go. And He was right. It was easier, now that she knew. I felt like things were clearer. I tried not to think about her, how angry she was, and what she had revealed to me, but that was like not thinking of a white elephant. Standing on a huge lime gelatin mold. That was full of cats. Hairless cats.

I hated cats.

We stopped for a break. She sat a little away from me; the distance was noticeably wider than when we usually sat together. I didn't push for conversation. I don't know if she was still mad at me or just absorbing the truth of what we had to do. I looked in my backpack; it was always emptier than Kate's. Her backpack always had things in it that meant something to her, like her teapot and that foul tea she liked. Whenever I looked in my backpack, I had what He had given me. A water bottle. Clothing to fit my surroundings. Sleeping bag when I needed it. And a large lacquered container resembling an elaborate jewelry box. I had not delved into the box yet, although the things that happened in Elysium had showed me that I didn't necessarily need to.

I did have one thing that was mine, something He had given to me. You know how when you were greedy on earth, people would say you can't take it with you? That's a lie-you can, as long as your specific deity thinks it's a good idea. At the bottom of my backpack was a small glass bottle with a wax seal. This bottle had sat in a drawer beside my bed ever since I moved to Tennessee. Kate found it once and asked me what it was-I'd lied and told her that I had picked up some sand from the last vacation my family had taken together.

I shivered – the air had turned thick and chilly, and the road was enshrouded in mist. "Great," I mumbled, disliking the sound of my voice here; I felt alone even though she was with me.

"Kinda feels far from Heaven, doesn't it?" she asked, and I was glad for her voice.

"I know. Colder, too. We should probably get going."

She finished her sandwich and stood up. I squashed a momentary fear of undertaking this mission and momentary guilt about lying to Kate. All right, these were not momentary. But I finally got to my feet and started walking, pulling the chain of the sign of the Traveler out of my shirt. I didn't recognize the symbol.

"

Kate, you know all the mythology; what's this supposed to be?" I asked.

She pulled out her own necklace. "That's Yggdrasil, the World Tree. A Norse symbol."

"So we're headed in the right direction. Good."

She chuckled. "You don't sound very happy about it."

"No, you're wrong, I'm thrilled to be walking straight into Ragnarök, the end of the world. Why would you think otherwise?"

She actually laughed, and my insides unclenched a little.

Voices in the mist caught our attention, but I couldn't tell how far away they were. They seemed disembodied and yet right next to me, and then thirty feet away, barely audible.

"What are you doing here, Old One?" A young woman.

"I came to learn, Urd. That is all." An older man.

A shout of laughter from an older woman. "You want to learn? I thought you knew all!"

The man again, amused. "I do not know how to purl."

"Sit, then. There is a little yarn left," said a third woman.

"Not much, though. Better hurry." The older woman again.

Then, we were upon them. They sat underneath a large respectable elm tree-a young woman about our age, a woman about my father's age, and a woman about my grandmother's age sat on a yellow blanket that seemed cheery in the dismal fog. A cloaked old man sat beside the young woman. He wore a floppy hat with a wide brim, perched oddly on his head to cover one eye. All four of them fiddled with yarn and knitting needles. The women were deft and

"

efficient, but the man knitted with no dexterity at all, as if his needles wriggled of their own accord.

Holy shit," Kate whispered in my ear. "I think that's Odin and the three Fates."

"Odin was what, the king?" I whispered back.

"Yeah, he's to the Norse what Zeus was to the Greeks."

"Oh. I guess you'd better say hi or something." She looked at me pointedly.

"Thanks a lot," I muttered.

"You said this was something you had to do. So do it."

Kate was more assertive now. I didn't know what to do about it. There was a hardness in her words, not cold, but I got a sense that I'd used up any slack I'd built up in our friendship and she wasn't letting me slide anymore.

I took a deep breath and raised my hand in greeting. "Hello, we're-

"

"Sit down, Daniel, Kate," the youngest said abruptly, and then smiled at me. She had red hair and brown eyes and had a serious, sexy librarian vibe going on. We joined them on edge of the blanket.

"I am Verdandi," the middle woman said. "My sisters are Urd and Skuld." She pointed to the younger woman and the older, respectively. "Would you like some cookies?"

"No, thank you," I said. Kate shook her head.

"Of course people had to show up to watch," the man grumbled. "The one time I lower myself to learn a woman's craft."

"

"Balls," Skuld said. "You knew they were coming, Odin. And you go and tell those fishermen who worship you that their knitted nets are women's work. See if you'll get another sacrifice."

"I haven't had a sacrifice in twelve hundred years, hag," he said. "And I have to keep face."

You and your face. I have no idea why you'd want to keep that old thing anyway," she replied.

Kate snickered, and Urd smiled at us. She pulled and unknotted black yarn from a burlap bag that sat between her and Odin. It went from her to Verdandi, who began knitting it to add onto a large afghan. She wouldn't get very far, though, because Skuld pulled out the stitches from the bottom as Urd knitted at the top, rolling up the kinked yarn into a fat ball. Other balls sat in a large shallow bowl behind her.

"I thought we would be entering a Norse afterlife, but it seems we're in Old Knitters' Heaven," Kate said, smiling.

"You, the herald of my doom, arrive here with jokes?" the man replied. "I guess he has the last laugh, as always, doesn't he?" "You knew he would," Verdandi said.

"Who?" I asked, but they ignored me.

"He'll be here soon, Odin, and you can ask him then," said Urd, looking closely at a knot in the thread before disentangling it. She raised her eyes to the sky.

I peered at Odin, who leered back at me and bared his yellow teeth. The skin around one of his eyes was puckered and shiny, and I remembered that he was one-eyed. Norse gods. What was the deal with them? I wracked my brain. I knew the myths were far more "depressing than most other folklore. Except for maybe the Japanese. I wished Kate and I could talk in private, but there wasn't much we could say at the moment, in front of the gods.

All I could remember was that Thor had a big hammer and there was that trickster god, a real bastard. Locki? Something. Managed to be both a mother and a father to some pretty scary stuff. I glanced at

Kate and she shrugged.

I opened my mouth to ask something – damned if I can remember what – when the ground began to shake. I was glad we'd sat with the foursome, as we certainly would have fallen otherwise. A horn sounded in the distance once the quake had ceased. It lasted a long time, cutting through the fog. Odin tensed, but the three women continued untangling, knitting, and unraveling.

"What the hell was that?" Kate asked.

"The sun'll go out next," Skuld said.

"What's going on?" I asked.

Odin glared at me. He opened his mouth and Urd elbowed him. "Daniel, dear, would you mind cutting this thread for me? I left my scissors behind."

I looked in my backpack and couldn't find scissors. My stomach sank when I realized what she asked. I pulled out the box I hadn't opened yet, the one God had given me before we left the Christian heaven, and lifted the lid.

Yup. Scissors. I'd expected them to be glorious somehow: made of gold with runes etched along the blades. But this wasn't Lord of the Rings-the scissors were simply silver with heavy black handles, like the kind my grandmother used to cut frozen mints. I handed them to Urd. She cut the thread and the sky darkened immediately. Kate gasped.

"What—" I blurted.

"The sun. I told you that, boy," Skuld said sharply. "Pay attention. None of this is worth anything if you do not keep your two eyes open."

Kate's face was white. "Wait. I remember. The sun goes out. Then the moon. Then-"

"The wolves are on the move," interrupted Skuld.

"Whoa. Uh, Daniel," Kate said, staring past me. "Your backpack is moving."

It was. I scooted away from it as it jumped once, twice. I reached my hand out tentatively and pulled it open. A fat crow flew out to the tree above us, where it pecked at a chattering squirrel and cawed loudly. Then it dropped to the ground.

I'd seen a lot of weird shit since coming to Heaven, but nothing like this: a hand burst out of the crow's breast, and then an arm. The bird split fully in two in a flurry of feathers as a grown man climbed from its interior. The bird skin, forgotten, lay at his feet, and he stretched naked before us. His scarred face grinned, and bile rose in my throat.

"Thanks for the ride," he said, hitching his head at me in greeting.

Kate's hand was tight on my arm as she whispered in my ear. "Oh shit. That's Loki - trickster, shape-changer. A real bastard. He's been imprisoned for hundreds of years with venom dripping in his eyes." Loki blinked, his wide snake-like eyes puffy and red-rimmed.

Skuld stood and fixed him with a glare. "You're not welcome here, trickster."

Loki slithered – he actually *slithered*; I didn't see his feet leave the ground – up to the woman and stuck his face in hers. She didn't flinch.

"I could gut you so you'd spill out like a pregnant mare's bag of waters, hag," he said. "This day is not marked by welcoming ceremonies. It is marked by war."

The horn sounded again and a deep, primal howl answered it, setting my teeth on edge and giving me goose-bumps.

"Fenrir, my son comes," whispered Loki. "Are you ready for your rest, All-Father?"

Odin ignored him and stood, his old body moving smoothly. He bowed to the women. "Ladies. It's been an honor. Perhaps some other time you can show me how to perfect this craft. I suddenly see merit in it." He bowed, and his knitting fell to the ground: a sloppy red square.

"All-Father, it's not always been good, but it's always been interesting," Verdandi said. Urd had tears in her eyes, but Skuld harrumphed.

"Get on with you, old fool. We all have our destinies."

He held out his hand. The youngest handed him the scissors I'd taken from my backpack. When the handles reached his gnarled hand, the blades melted together and elongated to become a spear with a black shaft. He hefted it briefly and tested its weight.

He nodded once. "It is good enough." He fixed his one eye on Kate and said, "Kate, It was a pleasure. And if I can give some advice, go with your first instincts." He turned his back to Loki and walked into the fog.

I felt breath on my neck and turned to see Loki so close he could have kissed me. I took a hesitant step backward. He held my waxsealed vial in his hands, the only possession I've ever cared about, and my fists clenched when I saw it.

"Megan trusted you to protect her. You failed her," he said.

"What?"

He didn't have a chance to reply. The horn sounded again, and more sounds came out of the fog: a snarl, the clink of armor, deep voices. The fog behind Loki darkened, a gargantuan shadow looming over him. It broke through the fog: a wolf whose size defied nightmares. Its fur was matted and its eyes ran with foul yellow stuff like a stray dog's. But this wasn't a dog. Not by a long shot.

Kate swore and I stumbled backward against her. We went sprawling, all the strength draining out of my limbs. The women stood under their tree behind us, silent.

"Father," the wolf said, his voice like a sword scraping across rock. "It is our time."

"Nearly," agreed Loki. "Daniel, we have work to do. I know what you carry in here." He tapped the bottle. "Pathetic. Why do you think you haven't seen her since you died? She doesn't want to see you."

He tossed my bottle above his head and it disappeared into the wolf's mouth with a crunch. I gaped as the wolf licked its chops. "Fear," it said. "It is good."

Loki reached up to an overhanging bough of the tree and snapped off a branch. In his hands it became a sword. "Now it is time. Let us go," he said.

He strode into the fog in the direction Odin had gone. The wolf leapt over us and bounded toward the sounds beyond that indicated an army's gathering.

I crawled forward, still weak from shock, until I found the neck of the bottle lying on the road, the part the wolf hadn't eaten. I closed my hand around it until it cut into my palm.

#

I don't know when my mother officially snapped. My father said later it was postpartum depression that just never went away. She had seemed normal, a little moody, maybe, but nothing to make me fear her. Then one day I came home from school to find her in the kitchen, crying about a broken computer and scrabbling in a drawer for a knife. She shouted at me to go outside, but I heard my sister Megan crying and I ran down the hall to check on her.

Megan hid in the corner of her room, clutching her blanket. I hugged her and told her it would be okay, that Mommy was just mad and she'd get over it, and that I would always protect her, but my mother was already in the doorway.

I don't remember the rest. Or, at least, I told myself, my father, the reporters, and the shrinks that I didn't. But the next thing I allow myself to remember I was in the hospital with cuts all over my arms. My father, red-faced and exhausted, was sitting by my bedside, grasping my knee because my hands were so bandaged. He said I was so brave for trying to stop her from hurting Megan. My mother was confined to an institution, later found not guilty of second-degree murder by reason of insanity. My father divorced her and moved us to Tennessee to restart our lives. Megan went with us, her ashes in a jar embossed with angels, with a small portion of her in a glass vial that I kept by my bed.

The cuts healed, eventually. I was in therapy throughout high school. I never saw my mother again; my last memory was of her staring blankly at me during my testimony. I told Kate she died before we left home, but she was only dead to me. She died for real four years ago. I did not go to her funeral.

I was only ten when it happened, but I carried the guilt of Megan's death for the rest of my short life.

Loki's words did their job. Ragnarök began, beasts and gods and monsters clashed on a field beyond us, and I knelt in front of the World Tree and cried.

CHAPTER TEN

I expected Kate to snap me out of my grief. I think I wanted her to. She'd always been there to hold me, even when I didn't want her to. But instead of her arms around me, a sharp kick brought me back. Kate stood over me, her hands on her hips.

"This is Ragnarök, Daniel," she said. "We have to be here for this. You can cry later."

Rage filled my throat so that I nearly choked on it. She was one of the most cowardly people I knew. Who was she to tell me to man up?

Then she extended her hand to me and I took it, her quick act of kindness taking the sting from her words.

A dirty rag hit me in the face. "Clean yourself up, boy," Skuld said. "You don't want to be remembered as the one who cried during Ragnarök."

I wiped my eyes with a lighter gray corner of the rag and wiped my nose. Kate watched me, unsmiling.

"Leave him alone, Skuld," Verdandi said. "There won't be anyone left to remember who cried here anyway."

Urd looked through the fog, frowning sadly. "They will all kill each other. It will be over soon." She began putting away the knitting needles.

Kate turned to Urd. "So there's nothing we can do?"

Skuld snorted. "Child, this has been prophesied for millennia. Fenrir will devour Odin. Loki and Heimdal will kill each other. Hel will arrive with all of the denizens of her realm. *Ragnarök* has come. Nothing will change that."

Urd made a sound, a strangled gulp. "No. Something *has* changed." She studied Odin's sloppy red potholder closely.

Verdandi took it from her and peered at the pathetic knitted square as if it were tea leaves. "Well. I never would have guessed. I didn't think the old man could surprise us anymore."

"Who? What has changed? What do you mean?" I asked.

Verdandi smiled at me. "If you had perhaps another millennium, you could learn how to read the threads. But Odin is a crafty god, and he wove himself a little destiny loophole."

I looked out on the field of battle, feeling helpless and hating myself for being weak, for failing my sister. And as with her death I was now destined to be a pathetic, useless witness once again.

I rubbed my face once again with the foul rag and took a deep breath. "I'm going out there. If there's nothing we can do, then I can't do any harm by trying to help."

"It isn't wise." Verdandi held Odin's red square to me. I took it without thinking.

Kate frowned and crossed her arms. "What are you trying to do? Remember what you told me? This isn't our battle. We're witnesses. Travelers. Nothing more." Despite her words, she looked thoughtful.

I took the square and ran it through my fingers. It was poorly made, with lumps and dropped stitches. "Ragnarök is all about the prophecy, right, Kate? Everyone here is meant to be here, everything that happens is predestined. Except," I continued, handing the square to her, "for whatever Odin wove out of the Fates' yarn. He made a change at the end. I don't know what it was. But I'm pretty sure we were not destined to be here, which means we can be part of that change."

I rooted around in my backpack for a weapon, a helmet, something. "I'm not going to be helpless forever, Kate. I couldn't help Megan when my mom killed her. But I can help here." I found nothing in my bag beyond my bedroll and the empty lacquer box. "Or I could help if my fucking backpack had something useful in it!"

"What, you think you can save him?" Kate asked me, still thoughtful.

"I have to try," I said.

"That big dog is Fenrir, you know. He eats worlds. He will eat gods. He may eat you."

I frowned for a second. "Look. God said I'd know what I needed to do, and I need to do this."

Kate chewed on her lip and then took Odin's knitting from me. She looked at one side, then the other. She glanced at Urd. The woman smiled.

"You see it, don't you?" she asked.

Kate's face gave away nothing. "I am not sure what I'm looking at."

"You are sure, girl. You just don't believe it."

Kate handed the potholder back to me. She walked over to the large metal bowl that held the balls of yarn. She looked at Skuld. "He'll need protection," she said. "May I?"

The old woman cackled. "You're smarter than I took you for, girly! Take it with my blessing."

Kate dumped out the yarn and that's when I saw the handles. It wasn't a bowl; it was a massive shield. She handed it to me.

"I'd go with you, but there's only one shield," she said, and smiled slightly.

"Hah!" Skuld cackled again. "You're not going anywhere, girl. You're staying here with us. We have things to discuss. The world will end just fine with the saner folk sitting on the sidelines."

I hefted the shield, wincing as I gripped it tighter and the cut on my palm stung.

Skuld shambled to me, age bending her. Her eyes twinkled. "Listen, boy. You don't need to fight. Just reach the All-Father. He'll be on the far side of the battlefield, incidentally. Look for the giant wolves."

I ventured a look at Kate. "I'll be back. I promise."

"I know," she said.

#

I'd never seen a real battle before. War movies seemed so choreographed; this was brutal and bloody and chaotic.

Odin was easy to spot. He stood well across the field, spear in hand, calling down lightning from the dark sky. In the flashes of light, Fenrir leaped and danced around Odin, impossibly tall, but kept at bay by the electricity. It was clear his hide was so tough that the lightning couldn't penetrate him, and it was little more than an annoyance. He bore down on the All-Father.

I couldn't watch so closely, though. To get to him, I had to get across the battlefield with my shield.

Giants, bigger than Fenrir, swung their great clubs, grunting and lumbering onto the battlefield, clearing the way of heroes and monsters alike. With a swing of their clubs, bodies went flying, spraying blood over the battlefield and creating a gruesome, coppery rain. They made their way slowly toward where I guessed Odin fought the wolves, and I groaned when I realized our paths would cross.

I took a deep breath and then ran, holding the shield in front of me, trying to reach Odin before the wolf got him. I couldn't see very well, and with more blood splattering around me, I raised the shield above my head for an instant.

I'd like to say the gods were smiling on me, but they were too busy slaughtering each other to notice. Regardless, I was able to stop short of running onto the side of a thrashing, dying wolf. Its body was a small hill to me, forcing me to run around it.

The giants were directly between Odin and me. I dodged the blow of a monster with three arms and way too many teeth, and raced straight for the giants.

They didn't notice me until I was right underneath them. Trying to remember what I'd learned from my one year as a failed junior varsity football running back, I dashed around the stomps and kicks aimed my way. I didn't notice the club though, as I couldn't see directly above me.

The club caught Skuld's shield, which sent me flying as the giant knocked me away like a golf ball. I held tight to the shield and closed my eyes as I flew through the air away from Odin, my stomach twisting with vertigo. Just as quickly, I realized I wanted to see where I would land, so I fought instinct and cracked them open again. From my high, soaring vantage point above the battlefield, I gasped, distracted momentarily from my fear by the sight of the blood, the monsters, the heroes, the arrows streaking below me.

I still held Skuld's shield. Miraculously, as the side of a hill drew closer, it slipped underneath me. I landed and the shield flashed brightly, absorbing most of my momentum. I rolled down a hill and came to rest, unhurt (though pretty sure I was going to puke), outside the battle.

"Damn. Handy shield," I said, shaking. I flexed my bruised but otherwise unharmed limbs.

I struggled to my feet and looked again for Odin. The air hissed as the sky opened and fire rained down on the field of dying. The battle had slowed, with more dead than live combatants. I held the shield above my head again and spotted Fenrir, the massive wolf, surrounded by cheering giants.

I was too late. Blood rained from his jaws as he devoured heroes and gods, silencing their screams as he tore them apart. My stomach threatened to rebel but I clamped my jaw shut and ran on.

Odin lay behind Fenrir, beaten and discarded. The wolf and giants moved on, the fire causing bright red patches on the giants' bald heads, and I was able to run past the groaning and dead, shield held aloft, to get to Odin's side.

Fenrir hadn't devoured him entirely; Odin looked as if he'd been chewed on, found too tough, and spat out. Gore coated him; the bloodsoaked robes, the pointy bits of bone sticking out of his shattered arm, and the blood that streamed from a severed leg did me in, and I turned from him and puked.

Unbelievably, he was still alive. Pale from loss of blood, but conscious. He fixed me with his one-eyed stare when finally I knelt beside him, shame making my face burn.

"Traveler. Herald of my doom. You're not the first to vomit on battlefield. May be the last, though," he wheezed, bright blood on his lips.

All I could think to do was comfort him. "You're going to be all right," I said, cleaning the blood from his face with the red scrap he'd knitted. My cut hand stung, and I hoped illogically that he didn't have hepatitis or HIV or something.

He coughed a laugh. "Don't lie, boy; you have no skill at it yet. I have known my destiny for thousands of—" He broke off, coughing again. Blood spattered from his lips onto his face. I ran the rag over it again.

"My son will kill the wolf. Loki will meet his doom. The world will end and begin again. In truth, it's good to be done with. You may be stupid, but you have done your job well." He blinked then (or was it winked?) and closed his eye. One more wheeze, and then he was gone.

"What did I come out here for, then?" I asked him. The spear had reverted to scissors beside him, so I picked them up. Better a lame weapon than nothing, I guessed. I wiped the blood, Odin's and mine, off my hands, and stood up.

Off in the distance, the huge Fenrir circled a glowing armored man – Odin's son? Despite the man's relatively puny size, the wolf looked less cocky and more careful. The fiery rain came down harder now; the scent of burning blood and flesh made my stomach turn.

I didn't see Loki, and I didn't recognize anyone else.

No, wait. I blinked, and the knowledge came to me like a tidal wave. I was glad I still knelt, else I would have fallen from the swoon that nearly took me over. I raised my head again, focusing.

Loki. Odin. The gods, the heroes, the Valkyries (one of them had supplied me with this shield), the monsters. I recognized them all.

Tyr, the one-handed, stood nearby at the bottom of a hill at the edge of a shimmering sea. I took Odin's floppy hat and covered his craggy, still face with it before I stood. "Rest well, you clever bastard," I said.

I walked down the hill and joined Tyr.

"She will arrive soon," I said, wondering at first what the hell I was saying with such conviction, and the knowledge hit my conscious mind immediately. He waited for a ship that carried his death.

He nodded without looking at me. His left hand flexed around his sword as his right arm carried his shield and protected his stump. He had not gotten entirely used to using his left hand in battle, even in all the years since Fenrir had bitten it off, but he didn't tell anyone that.

But I knew it. I knew it as well as I knew all the names of the gods in the field above me, the prophecies of how they all were to die, and what would happen after Ragnarök.

Tyr waited for Hel, goddess of the underworld, and her people to arrive by boat. He would battle with Garm, the guard dog of the underworld. They would kill each other; Tyr's sword in the dog's heart with the dog's jaws latched onto his neck.

"Be strong, Tyr," I said. I felt slightly ridiculous, but I patted him on the shoulder and he nodded to me again, grateful for the contact. A sail appeared on the horizon, and I left him there to his fate. I knew now I wasn't supposed to go on the battlefield to save Odin. I went there so I could bring something back. I returned to Yggdrasil, the World Tree, where the three fates and Kate sat talking.

Kate looked up when I approached. She smiled, unsurprised to see me. "Did you do everything you needed to do?"

"I'm okay, none of this blood is mine, thanks for asking," I said.

She laughed. "I knew you'd be fine, Daniel. I have been talking to the Fates while you were gone. But I'm glad you made it through."

The irritation loosened in my chest. I wiped some of Odin's blood from my face and hands, then handed Skuld her shield back. "Thank you," I said. "I'm sorry, Odin died."

The old valkyrie laughed in my face. "You say it like we expected you to save him."

"Didn't you?"

"Of course not. If you turn a gear slightly in a clock, it doesn't look like you've made much of a change, except that it moves another gear, and that moves another gear, and so on. Only one thing happened here than was not prophesied. And perhaps that is all we needed." I nodded slowly.

"I was with him when he died," I said absently. "I did what I needed to do. I think." I looked at my hands, the two-eyed perspective seeming slightly off to me. Something inside me expected only one eye.

I blinked, snapping out of my disorientation. "Did you see the battle?"

Skuld smiled. "No, boy, we had work to do. We were summoning the Valkyries. They should be here soon."

I looked from her to Kate, who had a small smile on her face. "The Valkyries?" I was about to make a clever comment about "ride of the" but suddenly I knew.

Kate told me anyway. "Legendary Norse warrior women. They visited the battlefield to take the greatest heroes to Valhalla, sometimes slept with gods or heroes, or sometimes just served them mead out of horns."

I nodded. "Did you summon them to clean up after the battle?"

Skuld harrumphed. "No, boy, the days of battle mopping up are over. The Valkyries, your friend reminds us, are unnamed in the final Ragnarök prophesy. There are many missing players in the prophecies regarding Ragnarök, stories that have not yet been told. They have a role to play in the aftermath."

She stood and took her shield from me. She still looked old, but considerably less frail. "Do you have Odin's spear?"

I handed her the scissors. "I am pretty sure I have more of him than that."

She winked at me and pulled a horn from the folds of her robe. "I have no doubt, boy. I do know if I were to take on my old role of leading the dead gods from the battlefield, Odin's body would be an empty husk. His essence remains with you."

Kate nodded slowly. "Wow. I really did read that knitting piece correctly. So he's there in your head?"

"His knowledge is; not quite his personality, though. Or he hasn't grumbled at me yet. I'm not sure." "Amazing," she said.

I grinned at her. "I think Skuld and the others can handle the rest of Ragnarök. I'm done here. Do you want to hang out any more?"

She looked over the battlefield, at the ghastly boat that neared Tyr's shoreline, and shook her head. "No, if you're good, I think I'm happy to leave."

We shook hands with the three Dates and wished them luck. We turned our back on Ragnarök. Skuld still blew her warning to her sisters, the horn echoing over the hills as we approached our small skiff to sail back to the crossroads.

"She'll be able to take the reins once it's all over," Kate said. "We talked about it. She's an amazing woman."

I leaned over the side of the boat to wash some blood off my arms and face. I looked up at her, dripping pink drops into the water. "So what did you guys talk about?"

Kate guided the skiff carefully. "We talked about the prophecies, the destinies, the Valkyries. They showed me some of their tricks with knitting, saying I had a knack. They've had amazing lives."

I rubbed my head, trying to choose my words carefully. I tried to sound nonchalant. "So, uh, why didn't you mind I ran off alone into battle?"

She shrugged. "I don't know. Odin told me to trust my first instincts. I figured you'd be okay. The knitted bit told me that he would be going on an unforeseen trip with a young man. So I took it to mean you'd be bringing him back, one way or another. I have to admit I didn't expect you to put him in your head."

She looked at me, head cocked. "So how did you manage to get him in there?"

"I have no idea. I just tried to comfort him, wipe up some of his blood, you know..." I didn't say *all the things I didn't do for Megan,* but I think she knew.

"Wiped up his blood," she said thoughtfully.

"Yeah." I looked at my cut hand, the edges already drawing together. The scars on my hands and arms were gone as well. Odin was the god of healing after all.

"

CHAPTER ELEVEN

I was finally able to break Kate's calm exterior and impress her with the fact that I owned Odin's knowledge.

"Can you name all of Loki's children?" she asked, challenging me.

I counted them off rapidly on my fingers. "Hel, Fenrir, Jörmungandr, Nari, Narfi, and Vali. He is also the mother of Sleipnir. The fact that I know how he is the mother of an eight-legged horse disturbs the hell out of me, by the way."

She laughed and shook her head. "I'm sorry, I'm just boggled. You always hated mythology."

"It's blowing my mind too," I admitted. "I feel like I need to go somewhere and just sit and have a good think. There's a lot of stuff in my head. But it's not like I have him talking to me. I think I just have his knowledge."

She laughed. "'Just.'"

"Hey," I said, trying to catch her eye. She looked at me calmly. "I'm sorry I had to run off into the chaos. I just… had to."

"It's okay. I understand what you had to do. It was another destined thing. I learned a lot about the Valkyries, Ragnarök prophecies, and even how to knit and read a little of the prophecies in the creations of the Fates. And hey- I knitted a bookmark." She grinned sheepishly and showed me a small strip of yellow fabric, loose but better put-together than Odin's first knitting attempt.

I fingered the soft yarn. Odin's knowledge whispered at me as I looked over her stitches, each loop a tiny hint about Kate, her past, and her future. I swallowed and handed it back to her, smiling weakly.

What is it?" she asked.

Nothing. You really don't have a future in crafting," I said, laughing.

She made a face at me. "You try to learn a new skill while the battle to end the world is going on in front of you, not to mention your best friend ran out into it!"

I held up my hands in defeat, giving up, and she laughed. The tension eased and she forgot, I hoped, the haunted look on my face when I had tried to hide what I'd read of her future on that strip of knitted cloth.

#

I was quite pleased I didn't have Odin himself in my head. I didn't think I'd want a crafty, cranky god trying to steer me to knit or go wolf hunting or something. But as we sailed, I flipped through the new knowledge like I had a large encyclopedia with me.

My thoughts about Megan came into sharp focus when I uncovered the information about Orpheus, the Greek bard who lost his beloved on their wedding day. The persistent bastard had gone to Hell – or Hades, as my grandmother and the Greeks called it – to persuade the god Hades and his wife Persephone for her return. They agreed to grant his request as long as he didn't turn around on his way out of the underworld, but the idiot looked back right when he got to the mouth of Hades, and she was lost to him forever.

Izanagi was another god - Japanese - whose beloved wife had died and who couldn't go on without her. Izanagi and his goddess wife, Izanami, had created the world, and then she died in childbirth. That seemed odd; she could create islands and gods, but a baby's birth is deadly?

Oh. More knowledge came through; her baby had been a god of

"

"

fire. Ow. That made more sense.

Like Orpheus, Izanagi went to the land of the dead to coax Izanami's return. Like Orpheus, he fucked up - his dead wife was well along the way of decomposition and begged him not to look at her. He did. She got pissed and chased him out of the underworld.

Izanagi was so heartbroken because of his loss that he killed his newborn son in retribution. I wondered what happened to that baby and what afterlife it could be residing in. Odin didn't know that part.

Lost in thought, I stumbled when the skiff finally hit the beginning of the "road" to Ragnarök. Kate and I jumped off and she headed for the sandy area of the roundabout.

"Lunch break?" she asked.

I nodded and accepted the sandwich she handed me. We ate in silence as I stared into the many paths ahead of me. I closed my eyes, trying not to think of gods, lost loves, and dead children.

"Daniel," Kate said, rousing me. I opened my eyes and she pointed.

Two old men dressed in shabby clothing and carrying walking sticks wandered down the road, waving to us. They grinned, their eyes wide in either madness or excitement. They seemed familiar, but I couldn't place them.

"Ho!" one shouted.

"Daniel! Kate! Liberators! So good to see you again!" One of them, the one with the long beard, grabbed my hand and shook it. The other tried to wring Kate's hand off at the wrist, he was so excited to meet her.

Kate looked at me, bemused.

I don't think we've met," she said hesitantly.

Might you have something to drink? We're terribly thirsty," the one holding Kate's hand said, eyeing her backpack. She pulled out a canteen and handed it to him.

"You don't remember us!" the bearded one said.

"Of course they don't," said the other. "No one remembers us. It was in the rules."

"Oh. But I thought they would... Ah well. Never mind. I am Isaac. That is my companion, Gigantus, also known as Mr. Big. We hoped we would find you before the end."

Isaac slurped at my canteen, water dribbling down his beard. "Heavenly. So wonderful."

It sounded familiar, but still I couldn't grasp the names. "Were you looking for us?" I asked as Isaac passed the canteen to Mr. Big.

"We have a message for you," Isaac said, wiping his mouth with his dirty sleeve. "We knew of your coming; it was foretold. Only a handful of prophets knew about you, but we have known of you since your birth."

"You're prophets?" I asked.

Mr. Big drank deeply without spilling anything. When he was done, he said, "You don't live as long as we did without learning a thing or two about the way the world works. We are prophets now, yes, but only became so after some years of wandering."

Isaac laughed. "Oh, but we had fun! And now we get to rest too. Just one more thing to do; one more message to deliver."

He lowered his voice, then, and leaned forward. "The big guy? He's using you, you know." He waved his fingers and hummed and then I realized he was acting like he had a puppet hanging from his fingers. "You dance for Him like little puppets."

"

That's the secret?" I asked, laughing. "I knew that. He sent us on the mission."

"But do you know why? Do you know what's happening now, at the time all the worlds end?"

"He's losing souls," Kate said.

Isaac scoffed. "And?"

Kate and I looked at each other and I shrugged. "Uh, and He's mad about it? Too busy to look for them Himself? Got too many meetings?"

"He's throwing down the gauntlet," Mr. Big said. "Armageddon, Ragnarök; all of the end battles force Him to sort things out. But He can't do everything."

I blinked at them. "I thought gods were all-powerful."

They both laughed. "There are still rules by which they must abide," Mr. Big said. "The worst part about YHWH is that He encompasses all gods. The Greeks have their harvest goddess and their trickster god and their goddess of the moon and the god of war and so on. YHWH must be all of these. So He's invoked during war and when people want peace, rain, sun, whatever, but He is also the trickster, the storm god, the fire god, the god of anger, and the god of death. He strikes a careful balance. He must have others help Him do His work. Others such as you, the heralds for the end times. Others such as us: well-punished yes, these two thousand or so years, but we chronicled human life past the birth of his son."

I smacked my forehead. "Of course, you're the wandering Jew and the Roman who struck Christ!" They both bowed.

But if you're here, then that means..." Kate trailed off.

That the end times have come to Earth, yes," Isaac said, his eyes still sparkling. "Our penance is over. We have been forgiven."

"Excellent—that means we're done!" I cried, springing to my feet.

"Oh, thank goodness," Kate said, sighing.

Mr. Big grabbed my sleeve with a tight grip, his face stone serious. "Don't be a fool. Your job is more important now than ever."

"Think, boy," Isaac said. "Why do you think He chose you? He is missing souls here."

Missing souls. In particular, one missing soul.

Shit.

"If you are here, then the world is coming to an end, right?" Kate asked.

They nodded.

"So traffic is going to start getting pretty busy around here," she said.

"It's going to take some sorting out. He's going to lose more before it's over with," Isaac said, snagging my canteen from where I had dropped it.

"How is He losing them?" I asked.

"YHWH is a god of order. A god of careful balance. Agents of Chaos are the ones disrupting things," Isaac said.

"Chaos? Like the devil?" Kate asked.

Mr. Big snorted. "Lucifer desires order as much as YHWH does. He has to process and punish according to the cosmic rules too. No, Chaos is a rogue force, it leaks into the world when there is a weakness or void. As we got closer to the final war, the foundations weakened. Chaos woke up. It started seeping through."

"

"It's your job to fix things," Mr. Big said.

I swore then, blasphemed, and caused even those who had beaten up Jesus to raise their eyebrows.

"Where do we go now, then?" Kate asked me.

I thought for a moment. Izanagi's story still gnawed at me, and I didn't know why. "Shinto Heaven," I said finally.

"It is as good a place as any. You'll go where you're meant to," Isaac said, shrugging.

"Then let's go," Kate said, then, to the men who had wandered for millennia, "I hope you get some real sleep soon."

Mr. Big saluted us. "We plan to. Good luck with your mission."

Isaac slurped from the canteen. How thirsty was he, anyway? He waved at us, soaking the front of his robe.

Now that we had some idea of where we wanted to go, Kate and I had no problem locating the dirt road to the Japanese afterlife.

"Isn't it weird that Isaac said He was using us? Do you feel like you're being used?" Kate asked.

"Not really," I said. "I feel like He needed a job done and He asked me to do it. I don't think He's got Megan locked up somewhere as a hostage or anything. Just that He knew I'd be... very motivated."

"Right," she said. "Well, at least we're not alone, right?"

I thought of the yellow strip of cloth she'd knitted, and what the Fates would say if they could have read those stitches. I smiled back at her and said, "No, we're not alone."

CHAPTER TWELVE

"Something has been bothering me," Kate said as we walked through the bamboo forest.

"Just one thing?"

"Well, every religion has its 'how the world got here' stories. We're discovering that all the gods seem to be real - but how can all those myths be true? You've got all that god knowledge now; do you know?"

I laughed. "Yeah, when you were a kid in church, you'd ask your minister all those question: about God and floods, or why your neighbor died of cancer, or why people who were mean got to be so rich while your dad, who was nice most of the time, couldn't pay all the bills every month, and they'd answer some shit about 'mysterious ways.'"

She rolled her eyes. "Tell me about it."

"Well, now I'm just realizing, as I go through Odin's knowledge, they were right. How could *all* of these gods create the world, each bleeding or shitting or birthing out land and sea? Well. They just did." She stared at me.

Her look was so incredulous that I laughed. "Man, I'd make a lousy dad. Okay, look. Here's how I am seeing it: you and me, we're walking and talking and meeting gods and witnessing battles and the end of the world and all this crazy shit, *and we're dead*. Since that's sunk in to me, I'm pretty much accepting anything."

"You're right," she said, shrugging. "I am still trying to deal with it all, I guess. Daniel, we saw *Ragnarök*."

"Of course, that does mean the world is ending," I said, shivering.

I wondered how it was going down back on Earth. My backpack shifted a bit. I hadn't been as comfortable opening it lately since Loki had jumped out of it, but I peeked inside anyway.

A newspaper. Thanks, God.

THE END OF THE WORLD? screamed the headline. Photographs of mushroom clouds dominated the front page. It seems that North Korea, India, Pakistan, Iran, Russia, the US, and China had all launched missiles at each other. There were no notes on the rapture, of people being lifted bodily into the air by the Almighty – He was too busy supplying me with scissors and newspapers, I guessed – and no notes on who the Antichrist had ended up being. Or who Christ had returned as.

I wondered if He had returned as a Jew or if he had converted to His own religion. The thought made my head spin. I decided I'd ask Him if I ever met Him.

With nuclear war reducing the world to rubble, the newspaper hadn't bothered to include a Lifestyle or comics section, so I stuffed the newspaper back where I'd found it.

"I seem to remember something about the Shinto afterlife," Kate said, flipping through a book she'd pulled from her backpack. Mist hung within the trees and an acrid smell entered my nose. I blinked and coughed; it was more than acrid, it overwhelmed me.

"Oh fuck, that's right. This isn't mist, it's wayward souls," she said, pulling her robe over her mouth and nose. "Don't breathe in."

I was about to make a sarcastic retort of how she could have told me that before I'd sniffed the stale air, but I was too busy coughing. I dropped to my knees, scrabbling for my backpack. I pulled out a scarf and wrapped it around my mouth and nose a number of times. Kate followed suit, holding her robe firmly to her face as she searched.

"Uh, what kind of souls?" I became aware of a presence in my mind. This wasn't Odin, because I hadn't absorbed his personality, just his knowledge. This was a definite other person; a quiet, pure mind.

Free her.

"What?"

"I didn't say anything," Kate said, then she turned white. "Oh, shit."

The end cannot come without her. She must be freed.

I wanted to ask, "Who?" but I knew already.

"We gotta free her," I said quietly. "Do you hear him?"

"Wait, what?" Kate asked. "Hear who?"

I looked around. Through the mist I could make out a sheer cliff face stretching up to an indefinite height. A young man sat perched serenely on top of a boulder at the foot of the cliff. He, too, had his nose and mouth covered, and he lifted his hand and waved when he saw us.

"Susanoo," I said, recognizing him with Odin's knowledge. "After Izanagi lost his wife, he just started making children out of his bodily fluids. Susanoo was birthed from his nose."

Kate made a disgusted noise. "He doesn't look like a god of snot." She was right; Susanoo was thin and strong, with shrewd eyes and a black beard and ponytail.

He leapt lightly off the boulder as we approached. He was taller than he'd appeared, and now I could see the katana that hung at his side. My heart rate quickened, but instead of fear, I just felt annoyed.

"Harbingers," he said. "Your coming was-"

"Foretold. Yeah. We get that a lot," I interrupted. He pursed his lips and slid his katana silently from its sheath.

Runes danced up and down its blade, which glinted silver or black, depending on the angle. Unlike Odin's shape-shifting scissors, this was truly a sword for a god.

"Then you won't mind if I dispense with the pleasantries," he said, and assumed a stance I recognized from countless video games.

"Hell," Kate said. "People don't seem to like seeing us anymore, do they?"

"If he says this is pleasant, I'd hate to see him rude," I said. "I guess it was foretold that you are going to gut us wide open?" I asked him.

He grinned with black teeth. "Most likely. We are to fight. The prophecies are unclear beyond that. I cannot let you move the boulder to free her."

Kate let out a breath. "Ohhh... Izanami. You're guarding the door to the underworld. I guess we're here to open it?"

The voice in my head, soft and high, spoke again. *Free her.*

"That's what the voice in my head is telling me," I said.

"How many people do you have up there?" Kate asked.

"So not the time to start talking about that," I said.

"This was the sword of the woman you seek to free," Susanoo said. "It can cut through anything. Wood. Metal. Water. The earth itself. Your very soul."

"Seriously, water isn't very hard to cut," I said lightly, dropping my backpack onto the forest floor. Kate did the same. "You should find another way to describe it that's more impressive."

He snorted and spat. "Arm yourself."

Through the wisdom of Odin I knew how to handle many weapons, in theory. I knew that there was more to fighting than swordplay; there was muscle memory and strength. I did not have muscle memory or strength. I peeked into the backpack; I also had no sword.

I looked at Kate, who sifted through her own backpack. She pulled out a small shield and made a face. "Not too helpful either."

"How the hell am I supposed to do Your work if You won't do Your part?" I hissed at the god who wasn't there.

Free her.

"Give it a rest," I said, then, to Susanoo, "Our sponsor doesn't seem to think we need weapons. Either that or He's playing a little joke on us. Are you going to cut down unarmed enemies?"

He answered me by raising his weapon above his head and shuffling forward, his weight centered low.

"Oh, shit." I backpedaled. Kate split left and I went right; Susanoo came after me. The first swing came for my neck, but I tripped backward over a bamboo shoot and went sprawling, the blade passing inches from my nose. It sliced through the bamboo like they were imaginary, and the thick trunks fell on top of me.

"Get up, or die with no dignity," he said, assuming his stance again.

"When did I say dignity was my goal here?" I asked. I lay there for a moment panting, as he was clearly patient enough to wait. The forested area got thicker behind me, where I'd be much safer. In front of me, past the mad god with the sword, was the clearing at the foot of the cliff, and the boulder that held back death, the goddess Izanami.

"Up!" Susanoo repeated.

I wrapped my hand around a slice of bamboo as I got up. I'd just seen him cut through multiple trees without effort, but it was more of a security blanket; I just felt better with something in my hands. The moment I regained my feet, Susanoo shuffled for me again. If I'd had a moment to think, I probably would have laughed. As powerful as he was, the shuffle step was hardly dignified.

Much like my actions in Elysium, I moved without thinking. I ran to meet him. Muscle memory wasn't there to fight him, but I knew enough about the katana to know where he would strike, and therefore how and when to react. His attack came low, this time, going for my legs. I leaped over the blade and couldn't resist whapping the god on the back of the head with my makeshift club.

It barely fazed him. I ran toward the foot of the cliff without looking back. Susanoo laughed, an ugly sound, and followed me. Kate also ran - I had no idea what she had planned, but I could use all the help I could get. He was faster than I was, and I nearly lost my head but I heard the sword whisper through the air and ducked in time. The blade nicked me, however, scraping across the top of my head. Hair fell into my face, followed closely by a thin stream of blood.

I was almost there. I reached the base of the cliff with the massive boulder that blocked the entrance to the Underworld. I put my back against it and faced Susanoo for the last time.

"First blood," he said, barely panting. "The next time I will not miss."

I panted much harder, the scarf around my mouth moist and hot from my breath. "I doubt you will," I agreed.

Kate stood in my peripheral vision, behind Susanoo. She held her small shield like a discus and winged it at the god.

I saw the sword come for me then, judged its arc and its power. It came at an angle, looking to shear both my head and arm from my body. The shield hit the god in the back just as he would have separated my head from my shoulders and as he stumbled forward, the blade buried itself in the boulder behind me, cleaving it in two. Gravel and dust rained down on me as it exploded and terror rushed out.

Susanoo stumbled backward, flailing. I tried to get out of his way, but the katana passed over my left cheek, nearly painless as it cut me. I heard Kate call my name.

I tried to blink the blood out of my eyes so I could follow what was happening, but everything was through a red lens.

The door to the underworld was open now, and the mountain vomited forth its inhabitants. Something spewed out: a cloud of flies that screamed one name with ten thousand enraged voices. "Izanagi."

Susanoo fell back, screaming. The sword fell from his hands as the cloud engulfed him. The cloud devoured him before the katana hit the ground.

I blinked again and then the pain came. The blood that obscured my vision did not come from my scalp, but from the left eye itself what was left of the eye, which wasn't much. I curled up into a fetal position, moaning, my ruined eye a confusion of pain in my skull.

The socket burned, a searing sensation that left me screaming. I forced my good eye open and actually saw fire dripping from my face, making the blood sizzle. I gasped, knowing I should be terrified of the great buzzing death that hovered nearby, but not caring. The voice whispered one thing, *Mother*, and then I knew the goddess was before me. Perhaps she could end the pain. I reached out my hands out to her.

The fire stopped and Izanami devoured me. Or I passed out in Kate's lap. I wasn't sure.

#

I awoke in the woods, lying on my back. The wound on my face was bound and the burns had a cooling cream on them. My skull throbbed distantly, as if I'd taken some powerful narcotics to forget the pain that was still obviously there.

"He wakes," said the voice. It was both soft and masculine, like a singer or a scholar.

"Tend to him," said Izanami. I didn't see her, but no one else could have the voice that sounded like a million flies screaming at once.

A young woman came into my field of vision, but she wasn't Kate. She was Japanese, traditionally dressed in a green and silver kimono, with her black hair bound tightly in a bun. She smiled at me and said, "Can you sit?"

I tried to nod, but the pain peeked its head in and threatened to return. With her help, I slowly sat up and looked around.

The woods had considerably less fog; a foul breeze came from the ragged hole in the cliff. Two beings, the cloud of flies that was the goddess Izanami, and a man made entirely of fire, talked to Kate some ways from me.

"Who?" I managed to croak.

"Kagut-suchi," my doctor replied. "The infant whose birth killed Izanami. Izanagi, his father, murdered him in retribution, and the child's soul has waited here for thousands of years, waiting for his mother to come for him. He held the pain of your lost eye until you had completed your mission."

"The voice in my head," I said, understanding at last. "And you are?"

She smiled at me softly. "Kazuko. Izanami is pleased with your service to her and her family. She has appointed me as your physician and guard."

I squinted again at the horrific death goddess. The flies had come together tightly to insinuate a woman's form, but she was still dreadful to look at. Kate talked to her as easily as if she were talking to a manager at a grocery store.

Kagut-suchi walked toward me and kept a respectful – and healthy – distance. He left ashy, smoking footprints on the forest floor. "Thank you for freeing my mother." He bowed low.

"Just, uh, doing my job," I said, feeling how lame it sounded right away. "Susanoo, what was he doing here, anyway?"

He gestured a fiery hand at the door to the Underworld. "The end of the world is nigh. My mother was the beginning; she gave birth to us all. She will be the end: the goddess of death. She yearns to take revenge on my father. Susanoo-no-Mikoto is his son, the storm god, exiled from heaven for dishonoring his sister in their longstanding rivalry. He attempted to regain his father's favor by keeping Izanami imprisoned. This slowed the end of the world. You stopped him. She is free. She can do her job now, allow the wayward souls to go home, and get her revenge on Izanagi when she ascends to heaven."

He bowed again. "We are indebted to you and hope that Kazuko is a gift worthy of the sacrifice you have given."

The woman bowed her head. I reached up and touched my bandages gingerly. If given a choice, would I have traded my eye for a traveling doctor? Probably not. But I didn't have a choice. Still, I knew the Japanese held honor highly, and the gods even more so than the people.

I bowed as best I could from my seated position. "I am unworthy of the gift; thank you, Kagut-suchi-san."

He bowed one last time and returned to his mother and Kate. "So she's going to do her part to end the world, then go kill her husband?" I asked Kazuko.

"She is death," the woman said. "Her path is clear."

I cleared my throat and thought of the dying Earth. "Of course."

"The small piece of a god you carry within you should have begun healing you by now," she said. "Do you feel any better?"

My head *had* begun to clear. Hope reared its ugly head, and I said, "Does this mean I will grow the eye back?"

She looked at me, her eyes kind. "Did Odin?"

I sighed. "Well, shit. Sometimes this job really sucks, you know that?"

"I am sure. Most do."

"Yeah, but most don't slice out your eye with a katana," I retorted.

"Hey, dude," Kate said as she made her way over, her forced nonchalance not fooling me in the least. "You feeling better?"

I glared at her as best I could. "Better than before, when there was a sword in my eye, yes. Better than five minutes before that? No."

She grinned at me. "You've reached the wounded tiger stage already? Excellent."

I looked away from her. "I'm not up for jokes right now."

She looked down. "I know. I'm sorry."

"No, don't be. I owe you my life, or afterlife, or something. If you hadn't thrown that shield he would have cut me in half."

She shrugged. "It was all I had. I wish I had done more."

I took her hand and squeezed it. "Help me up?"

She pulled me to my feet and I leaned on her, the pain in my head blooming anew from the altitude change. "I talked to Izanami and her son. Freeing her was our big goal here, and opening up the underworld. The mist around here was all the souls who haven't been able to go to the underworld since Izanagi blocked it at the beginning of time. Now they have somewhere to go, and Izanami is free. And you've met our bodyguard?"

"You mean my doctor?" Kazuko had been silently sitting up to then; she stood and straightened her kimono. Her sword, a straight Chinese blade, came into view, and I thought about how useful she would have been about half an hour before.

I put a hand to my head. The pain had receded and I knew I'd be healed, as much as I could, in a couple of hours. Kazuko looked into the now-open tunnel to Yomi, the underworld.

"I hope I don't have to warn you that going there in search of your sister would be a tragic journey," she said.

"Is she there?" I asked.

Her calm gaze met my eye. "No."

"Well, then. Let's go."

We stopped to bow to the goddess of death and the god of fire before leaving the Shinto afterlife. They bowed back, thanking me once more.

We walked in silence. Kate broke it finally by saying, "That was... intense."

I snorted. "Understatement of the afterlife, Kate. Nice place. We've lost our dog, what I had left of my sister, and now my fucking eye," I said as the world reverted back to the standard, bland, landscape. "I nearly lost my best friend; what's next, my balls?"

Kate looked at me directly. "You won't lose me, Daniel. I've got your back, remember?"

Her frank words made me flush, and I looked down.

Kazuko spoke up from behind us. "Izanami died of burns when she birthed Kagut-suchi. She retreated to Yomi where her body and soul were devoured by beetles, maggots, and *kaku*. Eventually all that was left were the flies that came from the maggots, strengthened by the essence of the goddess within. She waited there for thousands of years, vengeance the only thing on her mind. Vengeance to him who dishonored her and looked upon her after her death when she had bid him not to, and on him who killed her son."

Okay, I guess that was worse than losing an eye. "Yeah, but—" I said.

"Izanagi sliced the newborn baby Kagut-suchi into eight pieces, each creating new gods and demons. The newborn's soul has been here ever since, waiting for its mother."

I tried to interrupt again. "I know, and I—"

She continued. "Millions of people on earth died in the first nuclear attack. Their skin melted and their organs disintegrated. When they enter Yomi, there will be nothing for the maggots and *kaku* to devour. Those who will die of radiation poisoning or survivor violence will get to rot in Yomi. They will scream as the beetles dig holes in their genitals and maggots devour their—"—

"Okay, okay, I get it! People have it worse off than me. Sheesh."

Kate glanced at the stern woman. "You must be a ball at a party."

She rewarded us with a tight smile and continued down the road. I was so tired. I wondered if Kazuko would just leave us if we sat down to rest, but Kate wedged herself under my arm and I leaned on her gratefully.

"I'm not really thinking clearly," I said. "Where do we go from here?"

She held me tightly around the waist and I marveled at her strength. "Let's get to the roundabout and decide then."

"There's not much left keeping me from dropping right here," I said, resting my head on hers.

"There's me."

"I feel like I could sleep until the end of the world." I whispered into her hair.

"Apparently, that's not too far off now," she said.

CHAPTER THIRTEEN

"Daniel, wake up," Kate said. I groaned and rolled over. She nudged me. "No, seriously. Get up."

I opened my eye and glared at her. She pointed down a road. "You wanted to sleep till the end of the world. Time to wake up."

I carefully rubbed my good eye and noticed the pain had pretty much left my head. The scars on my face had faded at least by touch, but eye was gone. Forever, I figured. Shit.

The road Kate pointed down was not one we'd traveled before. I'd never considered that one of the roads would lead back to Earth, but clearly that's where this simple dirt road led, as souls began trudging toward us. Only a few led, but a darker mass on the horizon indicated they were not alone by far. I stood up to see if I could see farther.

"Why haven't we seen souls on the road before?" Kate asked, joining me.

Odin's knowledge bubbled up in my head. "There are more than one road to heaven. It's meant to be a solitary journey. But apparently even metaphysical roads aren't infinite. They're overwhelmed with souls. I mean, we had, what, six billion people?" "More than that," Kate said.

The mass of people neared us, hollow-eyed souls who barely looked right or left as they passed the roundabout and went unerringly toward their own heaven.

"I wonder if they see the roundabout," Kate said. "I didn't see it when I died. Did you?"

"No," I said. "I think their road goes where it's supposed to. I'm not sure they even see us."

So of course I had to be proven wrong when three souls wandered past and turned, focused on us, and then charged.

We had camped in the soft sand in the center of the roundabout, about ten feet from the road. The souls looked like regular humans, but regular humans who were undergoing some horrific torture. One man with knives through his eyes lunged for us with a third knife, apparently not needing the sight he'd been robbed of. My face twitched, more disturbed by the gruesome reminder of my loss than the actual attack.

A woman, her long hair ablaze, tried to use herself as a weapon, launching herself at Kate, her screams nothing but tortured grunts as her vocal cords melted.

The third looked as if it were a garden-variety zombie, rotting flesh dripping and maggots writhing. It moaned and belched a noxious cloud.

All of this I processed after the fact. What really happened was that while Kate and I stood and watched our doom approach, too stupefied to react, Kazuko jumped in front of us. Kate shoved me down and sand flew into the air, and then Kazuko went to work.

Her sword was out instantly. She assessed the threat and cleaved the burning woman in half just as the demon reached Kate. Then the knife-man lost his extending arm in a spray of blood. A nasty sound came from the zombie and Kazuko bent her legs, wrapped her arms in tight, and hit Kate like a small, dense battering ram. She fell over me just as the cloud passed over our heads. Kazuko dropped, rolled, and was up in an instant. She went immediately from a small, compact ball to a wide-stretching, graceful crane, and the zombie's head landed ten feet away on the edge of the roundabout and bounced into the road.

Just for good measure she beheaded the flailing knife guy, and then calmly wiped her blade with a handkerchief.

I panted in the sand, looking up at her, then at the remains of my assailants, then to Kate, who was as startled as I was, and then back her.

"I believe the borders are fracturing," she said, scrubbing some soot off her blade. "The rogue beings that exult in chaos have discovered your quest to stop them."

Something within me snapped. I scrabbled to my knees, rooting through my backpack and yelling. "Give me something. Anything. If You will not protect me, give me something to protect myself. Damn You, give me something!"

"Daniel-" Kate began, but I snarled at her as I found a tiny pocketknife at the bottom of my backpack.

I stared at it and hurled it down an empty afterlife road. "What? Don't like the fact that I swore at You? That's one of the Ten Commandments, right? No killing, no coveting, no swearing, and not holding other gods before You? But all I've been doing is finding other gods, several of whom have helped me out a ton more than You have. You have me run from gods with swords without giving me one. You have me lose my fucking eye. I'm like Your fucking leashed lapdog, and I don't even know if I'll get what I want at the end, because You don't know where Megan is!"

I gripped my head and howled. The socket where my eye had been throbbed; it had taken longer to heal than I had expected, but then again the stress of the attack and my rage might have inhibited the healing process.

I grabbed the backpack and threw it after the knife. "I've had enough of this!"

Abruptly I realized I was being watched. Kate stared at me as if she didn't know me. Kazuko stood quietly beside the three assassins. She had replaced the straight blade in its sheath, but held a familiar object in her hands.

"Where did you get that?" I asked, willing my voice not to shake.

She held Izanami's katana, taken, I assume, from the no-longerwith-us Susanoo. "She wants you to have it. If your god will not give you the tools in which to protect yourself, then she will aid you."

"I don't want it." I touched my bandage involuntarily.

"The tool is not to blame for what its wielder does," she said.

I had been complaining about not having a weapon. Now that I had one offered I didn't want to touch it. I stared at the hated sword. Kazuko unsheathed it and the runes glinted on the blade. In her hands, it looked like pure silver, with no shadows of malevolence. In my mind, Odin's knowledge played through all of the proper ways to use the katana, what was forbidden according to bushido, the warrior's code, and the history of the blade. For a craggy old man, he sure did know a lot about the weapons of a different culture.

"Do you know how to use it, Daniel?" asked Kate. "Anything in Odin's database?"

I nodded, not taking my eyes from the hated sword. "I know how. In theory."

"Then take it. Two people with swords will suit us better than one, and I'd probably cut my own foot off if I tried to use it."

I shook my head. "Not now. I can't do it now. I can't even get used to having a blind side yet."

"You will never get used to that," Kazuko said, sheathing the blade. "You will learn to adapt, but you will miss it your whole life."

I laughed suddenly, the idiocy of my existence hitting me. "Yeah, but I'm dead."

She stared at me for a moment, and a smile crossed her lips. "You are correct."

Kazuko put the katana on her right side, opposite her Chinese sword. Kate offered me a hand up. I accepted it and brushed the sand off my jeans.

Kate gently adjusted the bandage on my face, a move of such unexpected intimacy I was stunned for a moment. And in that stunned moment when all I saw was her and her ministrations, I realized what we needed to do.

"We need to go back to heaven. Our first heaven," I said, and she smiled at me. Kazuko bowed her head slightly. I was tired of this. We needed answers.

#

I'd forgotten about that whole end of the world thing. It's easy to do so when it's not so immediate, when you have your own problems, like ancient gods fighting around you and with you, or throwing scaryass demons at you. But the bombs kept dropping on Earth, which meant that people were dying by the millions.

Heading back to heaven, however, was easier said than done. Kate consulted a book from her backpack and said that nearly two billion souls would be wandering past us (and then amended that she didn't know how many were going to end up in Hell). But we did not have the luxury of time, we needed answers, and it was clear the afterlife was not handling the influx of souls well.

The road became clogged with the souls of the innocents lost in the wars happening down on Earth. Children, mostly, toddlers to teens, all plodding along. They stared ahead, purposeful, without fear. They were all Japanese, many of them heading back toward the Shinto afterlife we had just vacated.

"Where are the babies?" Kate asked. Kazuko pointed above us where angels filled the sky, each bearing a child.

"The innocent are processed first in times of great death," she whispered. "They are the easiest."

The silence unnerved me. Children were not supposed to be that silent. "Is something wrong? Why are they so quiet?"

"A child's soul is not prepared for quick and violent death. They are so full of life that it takes them time to adapt. They are in shock."

My skin crawled as the roads became even more crowded, the children shuffling patiently down their proper roads. Some paths were more occupied than others. Unlike when Kate and I started, suddenly it was simple to discover which road led where, simply by following the children of different races and cultures.

Angels appeared in the sky, first as little dots then as larger, winged adults to land softly by the roadsides, glancing at clipboards and directing the children. Despite the crowd of thousands, maybe millions, counting the babies above us, the process rapidly improved. It was weird to see mine and Kate's private place, as I realized I'd come to view the roundabout suddenly too crowded.

I touched Kazuko's robe briefly and she stiffened. I withdrew my hand quickly and pointed instead to something shiny. "What's that?"

It hovered at the side of the road, uncertainly, until a small brown girl with glowing white hair picked it up and put it into a basket. She searched the road until she caught sight of another and snatched that one as well.

"That is an unborn soul of the Hindu people. That girl is an Angiris – an angel that watches over sacrifices," she said.

"I guess there's not much sacrifice to watch over right now, huh?" I said. She nodded.

"God, did we cause that?"

Kate stared at the souls of the dead, thousands of them, possibly millions. It was hard to comprehend. She held her hand to her mouth and pressed, the knuckles growing white.

"Kate, remember, it was going to happen with or without us," I said, putting my hand on her shoulder. "We had to be there to save Atalanta, and preserve Odin, and release Izanami. We didn't make this happen, we didn't kill them."

She walked to the edge of the roundabout and stood, slightly elevated, her head bowed. I made a move to go after her, but Kazuko stopped me.

"Wait."

"What?" I kept my eye on my friend, scanning the crowd of children, white-faced.

"She needs to process this information. She feels responsible."

"And I'm responsible for her. This is one reason I didn't tell her in the beginning."

"Still, we can't lose her in this crowd. She is tall and white. And besides, she is your best friend and will glow like a beacon in the dark for you." I didn't have a chance to ask what the hell *that* meant; she pointed to the children. "Look at the souls. Learn what you can."

I acquiesced and watched in growing fascination as angels from every religion gathered the unborn souls. Some females opened skirts and placed the souls beneath them. Others put the souls into bags. One African man carefully placed each soul into a different carved box and placed it into a cart. He did not have many boxes.

It was clear we wouldn't get anywhere through the mass of children. I shifted from foot to foot, watching them. "How long do you think this will take?" I asked Kazuko.

She stared at me. "Billions of people will take a considerably long time to process."

Another angel had landed at the roundabout, carrying a clipboard. She had drab curly hair and a long nose. Clearly a Christian angel, she wore a yellow cardigan over her holy robe and wings. She fussed around the roads, picking children out and putting them on the right roads, muttering to herself all the while. She checked her clipboard constantly. Other Christian angels looked to be in charge of the unborn souls; she just directed everyone else.

I tried to remember if I'd seen her before, but I couldn't place her. Perhaps I'd seen her on my own trip to Heaven. The first time, I mean.

Kate had noticed her, too, and was headed straight for her, gently pushing uncomplaining children aside as she made her way.

Kazuko watched, her back straight and her face serene. "Something is wrong here." She spoke as if commenting on something funny her mother had told her that morning.

"What do you mean?"

She gave me a withering look. "Do you ever use that wisdom inside of you or are you just saving it for a rainy day?"

"If you know so much, then why aren't *you* doing God's work?" I said.

"I am doing the goddess's work. Isn't that enough?"

I glared at her and looked back toward the road, sighing. Children still came from the one road into Heaven and were sorted and directed down their proper road. Unborn souls drifted along until someone rescued them. My eye kept drifting back toward the officious angel and her cardigan. Ridiculous earrings swung from her ears, little blue globes on small chains. Every time she turned her head they banged against her neck and jaw - they did so even as Kate put her hand on her arm, getting her attention.

Something about the angel pulled at me. Something yearning and terrible wafted from her like the stink of a stable clinging to a farm hand. I gasped. Kate knew it before I did, but unfortunately Kazuko and I were armed and she was not.

I had known Kate would be leaving me; the fate she'd knitted in the yellow scrap had told me that much. Only I hadn't known how, or when. If I had known, perhaps I could have stopped it. But prophecies don't work like that.

I approached the road, not caring if Kazuko was behind me or not. The children were nearly impossible to get through; they didn't part for me like they had for Kate. While Kazuko and I struggled, Kate yelled something at the woman, grabbing the front of her cardigan and pulling it open.

Dozens of small spikes covered the angel's naked, sexless torso, upon which several golden souls were impaled. They made no noise and did not move, but I knew that each felt unbearable pain. I could *feel* them, and then realized Kate had felt them too. I stopped in revulsion and Kazuko made a choking sound as she pushed past me.

Kate looked at the angel in horror, frozen in place. The angel grinned and stepped forward, her outstretched arms winding around Kate. I choked out something and renewed my efforts to run forward. The angel's wings flexed as her horrific body pushed against Kate, the glistening spines pressing through her clothes into her body.

Kate fought. My friend struggled and grunted, gasping as the spikes drove deeper with each flex of her attacker's wings. With a cry, she closed her eyes and then the Kate that was Kate, her physical being, dissolved and drifted away on the wind.

Nothing remained but one more shining soul, impaled on a spike. Kate was gone.

I roared something unintelligible and shot forward, the children scattering suddenly. Where I had before assumed they were dazed and not aware of their surroundings, the children now moved away from the roundabout as a crowd, creating a space around us. Many pushed the unborn souls away as well, protecting them. I was only dimly aware of this.

The angel actually bared her teeth as she saw us coming. Kazuko had pressed the katana into my hand, and it felt natural to me; unnervingly so.

We had nearly reached her, swords drawn, but the angel smiled and moved her hand toward her right ear. Kazuko and I both struck as the angel grabbed her earring and squeezed it.

The blinding light seemed to flare a long time before the roar of the explosion, but I'm pretty sure, in hindsight, that they were simultaneous.

As consciousness left me, I wasn't sure if our swords had reached her or not.

CHAPTER FOURTEEN

After all we'd been through, I'd planned on confronting Him with more panache. I'd gained the wisdom of a god, lost an eye, outwitted other gods, and now carried the sword of a goddess.

In the imagined confrontation, I hadn't planned on going the way of Lucifer or anything, or even simply arguing that God perhaps was doing a bad job. I just wanted to know what was up. I wanted all the information. I finally understood why Kate was so freaked out when she saw the souls. We had lost enough, felt responsible for enough, and for what?

But no, I was not permitted to confront Him with righteous anger and fury. I instead appeared naked inside His study, feeling ethereal, as if I'd been formed of mist only seconds before.

I opened my eyes and saw Kazuko tying the sash of a white kimono. Before I could react and cover myself, angels slipped a robe over my shoulders and a white band across my ruined eye.

God stepped back and smiled at me. "There. Back together again."

"What happened?" I asked. "Where's Kate?"

"You found an agent for the adversary, as I'd hoped you would do. She had a discarnate explosive that she used when you figured her out. The three of you disintegrated. I have put you back together." He looked pleased with Himself.

"So where is Kate?"

"When I said, 'the three of you' I meant the agent for the adversary, you, and your guardian. Kate had already been discarnate, and the attack on her did a great deal of damage to her soul."

"I don't understand - can't You put her back together like You did us?"

"The end of the world is a busy time for Me," He said, still serene. "Souls are still slipping through the cracks. I need you more than ever now, to discover where the new souls have gone and retrieve them."

"Wait, we found the rogue. We started the end of the world in every afterlife we reached, except for maybe Dog Heaven. We have done what You asked. And You can't bring her back?"

"Your damage was to your bodies. Kate's damage is to her soul. I could give her a body again, but her soul is still damaged. To repair that damage takes more power than I can to expend right now."

"This is bullshit!" I said, rubbing my face. My fingers caught on the white band over my eye and dislodged it. "We did everything for You! And You can't even-"

I gasped and pulled the band down. My healed eye blinked ferociously in the light, acclimating to it. "Wait, why is my eye back? I thought that couldn't be healed?"

He looked down. "When you became discarnate, you lost that which was within you. I was able to restore you whole, however. You are as good as new."

"Wait a minute, I lost *Odin* too?" Nausea stirred in my belly, although I couldn't remember when last I ate. "And Megan is still gone?"

The anger that gathered in my chest dissipated at the sorrowful look on His face. "Yes. I am sorry, Daniel."

"I thought You were all-powerful! So what's with You not giving me any help out there? I had more help from the Norse and the Japanese than you. Did I fail some test, or give into temptation or something?" I was horrified at the realization that my hard-won anger had given way to threatening tears. So not the first way I wanted to use my new eye.

God shook His head. "Not in the least. My children have free will. I wanted to see how you would go about the adventure. You were taken care of, don't you think?"

"Kate hasn't been."

He went to the mantle and pulled down a bottle I hadn't noticed. Glowing yellow liquid swirled within. I swallowed. "Is that her?" I asked, my voice barely a whisper.

"Kate's substance is less ethereal and more chaotic, damaged as she was by an agent of chaos. This damage is different from what I am used to; her dis-incarnation was quite traumatic. At this moment, as is perhaps obvious by the missing souls, I am not fully omnipotent. The fracturing of My power has taxed Me greatly. If I were to give her a corporeal body, I am afraid her soul would leak out and dissipate."

I stared at the bottle in anguish. "But, You're God aren't You? You fixed us, so fix her!"

God placed the bottle on the dais and looked at me. "The afterlife is too chaotic now for Me to use the power I have to assist her."

He frowned at me, His face so sad I could barely look at it. "The truly tragic thing here is that I am not the only god who has the wisdom to repair damaged souls." *Oh shit.*

"Odin," I confirmed.

He nodded. "I am sorry, Daniel."

He left the study. I sat there with the silent Kazuko and the ruined soul of my best friend. And my two eyes.

And my little, mortal, stupid brain.

CHAPTER FIFTEEN

The shattered soul of the being who was once named Kate watched the man crumple and weep. The woman watched him, too. The soul wondered why the woman didn't comfort the man; she just sat there. That wasn't nice. A winged woman entered the room and handed the woman two swords. She stood and took them, bowing to the servant. She strapped one sword around her waist and one across her back.

She approached the man at last and pulled him up to a standing position. She picked a white band off the floor and efficiently wiped his face. He took it from her and stuffed it into the pocket of his robe.

He picked up the soul's bottle, then, giving the soul a thrilling ride as it swirled within its confines. He looked at it, tears brimming again, and then gently put it back down on the mantle.

They left, then. The soul was disappointed; but it somehow knew the man and woman had saved it from the searing pain from before. It remembered nothing before the searing pain. It would have liked to push its way out of the bottle, but one needed a body for that.

It dozed for a bit, having nothing to occupy its interest. A couple of angels entered the room, frantically switching reality around. The walls fell away, the roof dissolved and the wooden floor of the study became the deck of a ship. The soul enjoyed the pitching of the deck, and eagerly watched more people appear on the deck.

The Great Being was there again, the kindly man who had gathered the soul and put it in this jar before it had melted away.

The Great Being stood on the ship, dressed in light clothing and a hat to keep the sun off his face, and faced two others. The two men were both in business suits without a thread out of place, well-fitting, and with looks on their faces of complete discomfort. Very Important Men, then. Leaders, perhaps. The Great Being spoke to them, turning the wheel of the ship, and they struggled to maintain their footing. In front of them, the sea writhed and churned. One of the men frowned and tried to speak, but the Great Being cut him off. The boat rocked and the men grabbed onto rigging.

The soul stayed strangely rooted to the deck of the ship, unaffected by the turbulence. The cause of the choppy waters became apparent soon enough, and the men screamed when they saw it.

A great whirlpool swirled ahead, sucking in all around it. The Great Being didn't fight the pull, instead he steered the boat so it would be caught in the current. The men both dropped to their knees and spoke to the Great Being, tears streaming. They traveled faster as they began swirling around the whirlpool. The Great Being paid them no attention, instead bending to pick up the soul and its jar.

As the ship descended, the men holding to the rigging desperately, the Great Being stepped off the deck and fell, landing nimbly in the study.

He put the soul back on the mantle, and it waited there for the next exciting thing to happen.

The Great Being met with angels who gestured and waved their arms about; once a stray and desperate wing nearly knocked the soul from its perch, but the Great Being steadied it. The angels spoke of things like fracturing and chaos and the hand over.

The soul wished it had hands. They looked like fun.

The Great Being frowned and stared at the floor. He then pulled a letter from his robe and handed it to an angel. They left the room together.

More time passed. The soul tried again to achieve some sort of corporeal body, but it couldn't manage so much as a finger.

More angels. More meetings. The soul began to grow bored. There was no concept of passing time here in this little room, and there were no more exciting boat trips.

It was during a meeting with some small glowing children that another exciting thing finally happened.

The man returned, the woman behind him, her face still unmoving. The man carried one of the swords now, unsheathed. He wore the same white robe, only now it was tattered, sandy and bloody. The soul wondered what adventures they'd seen. The man turned to look at the soul, and the injury to his face was suddenly apparent: he had lost his left eye, the socket and three deep scratches covered by the white rag he'd used to wipe his tears earlier.

He spoke quickly to the Great Being, his hand white with the effort of gripping his sword tightly, the muscles in his jaw clenching.

The Great Being accepted this interruption in stride, dismissing the children and standing to meet the man. He touched the man on the shoulder and smiled, and the man relaxed his grip. The woman knelt by the door.

The Great Being sat the man down and they talked for a long time. The man's remaining eye widened as the Great Being talked, and he nodded slowly. The Great Being smiled one last time at the soul in its jar, and then left the room.

Choose a life to return to. Choose a body. The soul was astonished to actually hear the voice. Images flashed by then: a baby boy, an old woman, a dirty male farmer, and a young woman. Animals, then, a mouse, a giraffe, a hyena, a fox. When it landed at last on a hawk, the soul swelled in excitement.

Please, Kate, the voice pleaded. The image of the young woman appeared again, with emotions to go with it. Love, longing, frustration, courage, compassion, independence. The young woman had had a good life. Her body was strong. While the animals presented fascinating possibilities, the soul realized that the limitations were too great.

I am Kate.

Daniel stepped back, his breath catching in his throat, as Kate materialized in front of him. He averted his eye quickly at her nakedness, and angels silently entered the room to robe her.

"Kate? Are you all right?"

"I – I think so." The soul that was now Kate again rubbed its new face. "I saw... so many things."

Daniel rushed forward and grabbed her in a hug, burying his head in her shoulder. "I'm so sorry I let you go ahead without protection. I wasn't thinking, and you were so upset. I thought I'd lost you. I'm just so sorry."

Kate stood still, staring at the opposite wall. "I'm not sure I remember what you're talking about."

Daniel raised his head to look at her. "You don't remember?"

She shook her head as he stepped back. "I remember that am Kate. You are Daniel. I remember that we are friends. And- and we died together," She rubbed her face again. "I'm sorry. It may take me some time."

The Japanese woman came up behind Daniel and stood by his side. She bowed low and said, "I am Kazuko. It is an honor to meet again the woman who drives my companion to such passionate acts."

Kate stared at her. "I'm sorry, I don't remember you either."

"That's okay, you'll remember," Daniel said. He turned to Kazuko. "I'm right, right? She'll remember?"

The woman shrugged delicately.

Kate made to stick her hand out, but then pulled it back and bowed clumsily.

"What happened to your eye, Daniel?"

He grimaced, touching the edges of the bandages that were spotted with blood. "That is a very, very, long story. How about some other time?"

#

The three sat in silence, content to recover from Kate's disorientation and Daniel's discomfort from his injury. They all looked up gratefully when the study door opened and a small boy came in.

Daniel's eye widened. "Ganymede. Why aren't you in Olympus?"

The boy, whose golden curls hung into his blue eyes, frowned at the floor.

"I am no longer needed," he said. "There were too many deaths at the battle of Elysium."

Kate raised her head sharply. "Who?"

Ganymede's eyes filled with tears. "My master, Zeus. The goddess Aphrodite. The god Hermes."

Kate gasped and sat back into her chair.

Daniel put his hand on the boy's shoulder. "I'm very sorry, Ganymede."

The boy shook his head. "I am instructed to bring this to you." He handed Daniel a pair of backpacks and left the room.

Daniel put the backpacks on the ground. "Where do dead gods go when they die?" he asked Kazuko. "All the gods of Ragnarök, Susanoo, now the Greeks. Where are they all?"

The woman smiled slightly. "The gods can never go away. There are merely reinvented."

Daniel put his hand on Kate's knee. "He's not gone, Kate, any more than you or I were when we died."

She covered her face with her hands. "Him, I remember."

Daniel removed his hand awkwardly and looked at her for a moment. Then he fiddled with the backpacks. He groaned.

"What is it?" asked Kazuko.

Daniel pulled out a tacky necklace from one of the backpacks. "Looks like we're going traveling again."

"This is not surprising," she said. "He requires you still to travel heaven."

Daniel opened an envelope he found under the gaudy necklace. He opened it and the color drained from his face.

"Not this time. We have to look other places for more missing souls.

"We're going to hell."

ACKNOWLEDGEMENTS

All the Kickstarter backers who made this possible, and believed in the project. Too many to name, I am grateful for you all.

Sneak Peek at Hell The Afterlife Series II

CHAPTER ONE

I'd had no concept of time or self when I was a soul. I remember casting about, watching the Divine punish world leaders (which is what Daniel and Kazuko had told me He'd done). When I lost form but was touched by the Divine, I was stitched back together enough to comprehend my surroundings, if not my own identity.

We sat, the three of us, in the study of the Divine. I could no longer give It a name as I fully remembered Its touch. It was beyond Man, beyond Woman. The face It wore was a mask so most souls could comprehend what they wanted to see. But there was no comprehending the truth. Such power It had, such wisdom. It embodied the qualities of every god and goddess I had encountered and It got me wondering: was It a mixture of all gods, or was It the spring from which all the other gods were born?

Theological arguments aside, we had a mission. Why the font of such power required us to undertake this quest was beyond me, but trying to understand Its will was like trying to drink from a waterfall. I could only drink in a little at a time.

Daniel handed me a backpack. I took it wordlessly and strapped it on. Kazuko rose from her solemn kneeling position. She pointed behind us.

"That is the way out," she said.

A door stood where there hadn't been one before, in the middle of the wall. A Greek symbol was etched on the door, and it took me a moment to recognize Omega.

Daniel led the way, with Kazuko following and myself bringing up the rear. The door opened to a dark corridor. "Great," mumbled Daniel.

I closed the door behind us and left us in the pitch blackness.

"What did you do that for?" Daniel snapped. He'd been distant since his initial outburst. I think my inability to remember much upset him, as if he took it personally.

"I don't know," I said. "Habit, I guess. Don't leave doors open. Grandma Melissa would always say flies would get in. Dogs would get out. Air conditioning would get wasted." I rummaged around in my backpack until I felt something flashlight-shaped.

I turned it on and slipped past the two of them in the corridor. "Let's go."

We walked for some time. My head still buzzed with my experiences, and for a brief moment I regretted not taking the hawk's form. The hawk would unlikely be worrying about the cold silence behind me.

"So when are you going to tell me what happened to your eye?" I asked.

Daniel made a small noise.

"Never mind," I said.

"No. It's okay." His voice had lost the edge it had gained. "After you... had your... encounter with that angel demon thing... some stuff happened."

"That's not telling me much." I didn't look around but kept walking down the corridor, which had shifted from a hallway to a stone tunnel.

Kazuko's soft, matter-of-fact voice floated up from the back. "After the altercation with the entity who attacked you, we were blown apart, God put Daniel back together: complete with his eye, but missing the wisdom of Odin. It turns out that God would need the All-Father's wisdom to restore you. Daniel then found a way to regain what he needed. He got the wisdom back, gave an eye in exchange, and you know the rest."

I stopped and shone the light in her face. She didn't wince at the sudden glare. "I'm sorry. Can you go over that again?"

#

The cave emptied onto a barren plain. Distant screams sounded from afar. We stood at the mouth of the cave and stared at the gray waste and the gnarled, blackened trees before us.

"So which hell is this?" I asked.

"It isn't hell," Kazuko said. "This is purgatory."

Daniel scowled at her. "And how the hell do you know that?"

"I am your guide."

He turned to me, sighing. "See? She is still doing that."

I didn't return his exasperated grin. I pointed as figures came into view. In the gray afternoon (what time was it, anyway?) they lit up the dullness around them. Embers danced between the flaming figures, and they writhed as they walked.

"Good Lord," Daniel said. "If this is purgatory, what is hell going to be like?" He swallowed. He apparently already knew the answer to his question; he had a god in him to tell him as much.

I was just me.

What was I doing there?

Kazuko spoke up. "Those are the lustful. The fire is burned from them as they prepare for entrance into Heaven. As soon as they are purified, they are permitted to wash in the river of Lethe and enter paradise."

Daniel snorted. "Paradise. Right. It was a blast, huh, Kate?"

I remembered the touch of the Divine. "It is all they could ever hope for. They will receive their reward."

Daniel's jaw dropped slightly. "Please tell me you're kidding. Don't you remember getting to heaven, how it was all smoke and mirrors? We weren't even together, but I found you and we left to explore?"

"Except we were sent to watch the end of the worlds," I said absently.

He snapped his jaw shut. "You remember that?"

I nodded. "It's coming back to me, in bits."

"But that wasn't my point. We agreed that heaven wasn't all that, and we left. And now you're buying into it?" "You haven't seen it," I whispered.

"Seen what?"

"You haven't felt the true touch of the Divine. Your view of it is colored by your anger."

"What, are you a fundamentalist now? What the hell, Kate?"

I tilted my head, trying to understand. "You carry a part of the Divine within you, Daniel. When you realize that, you'll understand."

"Gah!" he shouted, throwing his hands up. He stomped out of the cave, heading toward the flaming walkers. Our guide, the stoic Kazuko, followed. I paused, and then walked in their footsteps.

The person in the lead, a tall woman in a flowing skirt, halted and bowed to us. Flames dripped from her hair, and her face twisted in agony, but she made no anguished sound. "Visitors to our hopeful land," she said. "What news do you bring?"

"Uh, we're actually on our way down. Can you point us the way out of purgatory?" Daniel asked.

"Way down? Do you come from the holy light of heaven?" the woman nearly wept in hope.

"Yeah," Daniel replied. "God sent us on a mission."

"Did He release us from our penance?"

"Uh, well, not so much," he said, shifting from foot to foot, looking at Kazuko. "What are you in for? I'll see if I can put in a good word."

"I am Gloria Francis Smoot," she said, bowing. "A prominent madam from New Orleans. My house of ill repute was notorious during the War of Northern Aggression."

"Dude. You've been here since the Civil War?" Daniel stared at her.

"Well, yes; that much time is needed to remove the taint of sin, or until the Judgment Day comes. And our day will come."

"What the fuck is going on!" Daniel yelled. He stomped around, flailing his arms. "Has the world gone insane? My best friend is a fundie, you're sitting here, *on fire*, spouting some shit about how it's okay that you're *on fire* because you'll be forgiven on Judgment Day, and you don't even know."

He stopped and grabbed her shoulders, gripping her burning flesh tightly. I winced in sympathy as his hands grew red.

"Listen to me," he said. "It's a ruse. Judgment Day was last Wednesday. It's over. Heaven is busier than Macy's on the day after Thanksgiving. He's forgotten about you."

She shook him off and took a step backward. Her compatriots shifted and glanced at each other through the flames. "Are you sent from Satan? Is this my final test?"

"You're not paying attention," Daniel said through gritted teeth. "We're not from there, we're going to there."

"You lie," she said. Her voice was barely audible above the crackle of the flames around her body.

"Really?" he asked. He pointed to the right, about one hundred yards away where an angel stood in front of an iron gate, staring at us. "Ask him. He probably can't lie, can he?"

A woman put her hand on Gloria's arm. "Do not despair, Gloria. You must keep the faith." Her friends crowded around her, making the individual fires grow to one great bonfire, and we stepped back, squinting.

"This is ridiculous. Let's get out of here," Daniel said.

We left them crouched and weeping. Daniel stalked far ahead of us, his spine straight and his fists balled.

"That was a pretty shitty thing to do," I told Kazuko. "He took away what remaining hope they had."

"Daniel is dedicated to uncovering the truth," she replied.

"How very X-Files," I muttered. I ran to catch up to Daniel and put my hand on his shoulder.

"We need to camp, dude," I said.

"What are you talking about?" he grumbled.

I pointed to the troubled sky. "It's getting dark. We're not in heaven anymore; apparently the other places have night."

We tried to build a fire, but couldn't find any wood. I thought about suggesting we convince a lustful soul to join us so we could see by their tormented light, but figured Daniel wouldn't find it amusing.

Kazuko stretched out on a light blanket, her hand on her sword. Daniel hugged his knees to his chest and stared in the direction from which we'd come, facing the fires of the weeping souls.

Memories sat in my mind like stories I'd once read but not experienced myself. I hesitated a moment, then went to him and sat down, my back to his, and leaned back. He relaxed against me.

"I am sorry I lied to you, Kate, and I'm sorry I let you go ahead to that angel thing without me," he said. His voice was tired, defeated.

"I never would have claimed my independence if it hadn't been for you, Daniel," I said.

"Still. I lost you for what felt like a long time. I really missed you."

I was silent for some time.

"Do you want to tell me about what happened?" I finally said.

"Can we talk about that later? It's still a little fresh," he said, and he shifted as his arm touched the bandage across the wound on his face.

"Sure."

"So why didn't you ever tell me you were in love with me?" he asked.

I should have felt nervous and flushed, but I wasn't. "Several reasons, I guess. I knew it would make things weird if you didn't feel the same way. And if you did feel the same way, we might someday break up and I'd lose all of you. And then there was the fact that I *did* tell you about a year and a half ago and you didn't return the feelings."

He turned his head, trying to see me in peripheral vision. "What?

When was this?"

"It was Christmas, we were hanging out at your house watching TV, the lights twinkling. It seemed like the perfect time. I gave you a love note with your present the next day, and you never said anything about it."

"Oh... Right. Hell, I was in love with ten different people a week back then. I didn't realize you were serious."

I snorted. "How much clearer could I have been?"

He didn't answer. I stared into the darkness, and I suppose he stared at the flickering, burning souls.

"What are we going to do about them?" I asked.

"Do?"

"Yeah. The tormented souls? Weeping and burning and all that?"

"Nothing. It's not our jobs to release them, we're just looking for the lost ones."

"I guess with all that god stuff you got, you skipped out on compassion."

He was noticeably still. I yawned, tired from returning to my corporeal body, and stretched out behind Daniel. I leaned against him, keeping contact, and fell asleep, with a nagging sense of something in my brain.

#

When I woke, Daniel was still seated, but his head was on his arms, and he dozed. Kazuko was seated cross-legged, making tea. I watched her pour water from a canteen into her teapot and the idea that had been nagging at me finally solidified.

I grinned and gently shook Daniel's shoulder. He raised his head and then winced and put his hand to his neck. He glared at me. "You are never, ever going to let me sleep, are you?"

"Not when I keep having brilliant ideas. You need to stay awake to keep up."

He groaned and looked at Kazuko. "Aren't you supposed to protect me?"

She didn't answer, but sipped her tea.

"Fine. Tell me, what glorious idea has sprung, fully grown, from your head?"

"Come on," I said, and pulled him to his feet.

All at once, it felt wonderful to have a body again, and I grabbed both our backpacks and ran toward the hill that the tortured souls surrounded. My feet pounded the ground and I outdistanced Daniel, who fell behind, complaining that his eye hurt.

I stopped short when I heard them, singing and wailing, calling out to God to remember them. I dropped the backpacks onto the ground and reached inside one until I found what I needed. I grasped the handle and lugged out a bucket of water.

Daniel caught up with me. "What the hell are you doing?"

"The Divine did not restore my soul, did It?"

He passed a hand over his face. "No, He made me do it."

"And how did you have the power do to something that amazing?"

"I got some Odin in a cut. What are you getting at?"

I thrust the bucket into his hands. Some of the water slopped over the side and got on his jeans. He swore.

"Free them. Forgive them. Release them."

He stared at me, his one eye wide. The souls staggered closer, recognizing Daniel. Their desperate faces turned angry and ugly. They pointed at Daniel and began running toward us.

The *ssssshhk* of steel coming out of a scabbard sounded behind me, but I held my arm out to block Kazuko. "Wait," I said.

She stepped around my arm and stood at my side, ready.

The flaming mob neared, and Daniel cast a look over his shoulder at me. "Are you serious?"

"Definitely."

He shrugged. "Worked for Dorothy." And with that he tossed the bucket of water at the mob.

With a hiss, the flames were gone. Seven wet souls stood in front of us, too shocked to go on with their planned evisceration of my friend.

The woman we'd spoken with the night before, Gloria, held her hand out and stared at it.

"There," Daniel said. I could tell he was much more nervous than he sounded. "Your torment has ended. You are free to move on to your paradise."

Gloria looked at the angel guarding the gate. He bowed his head and stepped aside, freeing the entrance to Heaven.

She flung herself, her very wet self, around Daniel's neck, weeping and thanking him. He dropped the bucket and staggered, clumsily returning the hug. They left him, after each hugging or kissing him.

Trying not to smile, I handed him a towel. He wiped his face and jacket. "You want to explain to me what happened?"

"I'm not entirely sure yet. I'm working on it," I said, putting the towel and bucket back in my backpack. "Till I figure it out, we have more lustful souls to free."

He frowned for a moment. "We're out of water. I'm sure there are more souls around here than that small group."

I stared at him. "Dude." I pointed to the bucket where he'd dropped it. It was upright and full of water again.

"How?" he asked, his eye wide.

"For God's sake, Daniel. We're in the afterlife. I created a house, garden, a fake you, and a relationship out of nothing but core desire. You think I can't dream up a little water? Give it a try."

"Wow, you think of everything," he said, sighing. "But you look like you need something."

I cocked my head. "What?"

"A shower." He flung the bucket at me. It drenched me immediately and I gasped as the cold water soaked me. By the time I'd wiped the water and my stringy hair from my eyes, he was running off, laughing.

"You utter and complete ass!" I yelled, picking up the bucket and running after him.

The bucket got heavier as I ran, and I looked down to see it filling with water again. Some fiery souls burned ahead of us, where Daniel was running. As much as I wanted to get him back, I remembered what was important.

****Please share the book if you like the content****

Read The NEXT series of Afterlife
https://www.amazon.com/dp/B08GSWR346

Printed in Great Britain
by Amazon